TANGLED WITH THE CEO

IONA ROSE

AUTHOR'S NOTE

Hey there!

Thank you for choosing my book. I sure hope that you love it. I'd hate to part ways once you're done though. So how about we stay in touch?

My newsletter is a great way to discover more about me and my books. Where you'll find frequent exclusive giveaways, sneak previews of new releases and be first to see new cover reveals.

And as a HUGE thank you for joining, you'll receive a FREE book on me!

With love,

Iona

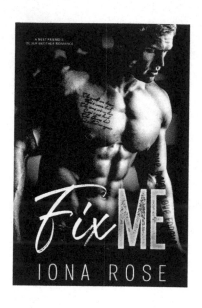

Get Your FREE Book Here:
https://dl.bookfunnel.com/v9yit8b3f7

Tangled with
the CEO

Publisher: Some Books
ISBN- 978-1-913990-20-6

Chapter One

CHANCE

I raise my glass in the air as the others do the same and then I down my rum. I get up and go to the small bar at the back of the plane and pour another one.

"Careful Chance," Sebastian warns me with a laugh. "You might actually start enjoying yourself."

I laugh along with the others, but Sebastian is right. I have a few things to do before I can let my hair down and enjoy myself this weekend. I take my drink back to my seat to sit down and watch the others for a moment.

Matt and Sebastian, my two older brothers, are playing some sort of drinking game, cheered on by Bradley, Mark and Rick, Sebastian's friends. It's his stag night and we're on our way to Vegas. I know I should be making more of an effort, but I just can't get in the mood until I know the few loose threads I had to leave at work are tied up.

In some ways, I admire Matt and Sebastian. They work hard, but they play hard too, especially Sebastian, although he's calmed down a little since he became a father. Carl is almost two now and fatherhood suits Sebastian in a way I never thought would be possible. I half wish I could be a little bit more like Matt and Sebastian. Just leave my work at the office and worry about it on Monday. But it's just not my style.

I'm not the sort of guy who can put off things that need to be done. They only play on my mind and niggle at me, where as if I can just get them done, then I can stop thinking about them. Except one thing always leads to the next and then I start thinking about that. And so it continues until my day off becomes another work day.

I sigh and shake my head. I don't know why I'm suddenly being so reflective. I like my life. I like being all about work. I love what I do and it's going to take more than a few nights in Vegas to convince me that I'm missing out on something more.

"Hey Chance?" Matt says.

I look up.

"It's a stag party, not a funeral. Smile or something." He laughs.

"Isn't it pretty much the same thing?" I ask. "Once Seb gets married, his life is pretty much over right?"

This gets a chorus of cheers and a laugh from Sebastian.

I grin and tell myself to forget work, just for a couple of days while we have the stag party and then get the wedding over with. I can always catch up on work and now isn't the time for work. It's the time to be a good brother. I get back up to join the others where they're still crowded around watching Matt and Sebastian play their drinking game.

It's a good thing we have a private jet, because I don't think a standard airline would take too kindly to this game. The only rule seems to be to sink as many shots as possible.

"What are they playing?" I ask, taking in the piles of shot glasses and the bottle of half gone Tequila.

Mark laughs. "I don't think it has a name. Maybe it should be called alcohol poisoning or something. They have to build a pyramid out of shot glasses. The first person to do it wins and the other one has to drink five shots of Tequila in a row."

It didn't look quite as lethal as I first thought, now I know most of the shot glasses are just being used as building bricks.

Matt puts his hands in the air and cheers when he sets his final shot glass on his pyramid and it doesn't fall over.

Sebastian groans. "Remind me again, why I suggested playing this. I suck at it." He laughs.

"Shut up and drink." Matt chuckles.

Sebastian shakes his head. "I've already lost two rounds. I won't see Vegas at this rate."

"Drink, drink, drink," the guys begin to chant.

I find myself joining in with them.

"Okay, okay." Sebastian grins, holding his hands up in surrender. He downs the shots one after the other, wincing after each one. He gets to the last one, looking like he's about to throw up. He chases it down with half a bottle of beer and moans loudly when he's done.

This gets him a round of cheers from the guys. He gets unsteadily to his feet and stumbles towards the bathroom.

An even louder round of cheers rises up with some laughter and clapping. It's obvious what he's going to do as he disappears into the bathroom.

Matt gets up and puts his fists in the air. "Reigning champion. Who's next?"

"Me," I say, surprising myself.

"No way!" Matt scoffs. "You'll be able to have the pyramid built in seconds. You do this all day every day."

"I'm an interior designer." I laugh. "What part of that involves building pyramids out of shot glasses?"

"Ah, you know what I mean." Matt grins. "Building stuff, designing stuff. It's all the same thing isn't it?"

It's not even close and I doubt for a second I would beat Matt at building the pyramid, but I'm not bothered about winning. I just want to get a bit tipsy and get into the same high spirits the others are in. "Okay." I grin. "How about we just pretend we played and you won and I'll drink the shots?"

"Really?" Mark says, raising an eyebrow.

"Really," I confirm as I sit down.

Bradley grabs five shot glasses and begins to fill them up with Tequila. He's onto the fourth one when Sebastian comes back out of the bathroom.

He still looks a little bit white, but he looks a damned sight better than he did before he went into the bathroom.

"Are you okay?" Matt asks him.

Sebastian laughs and nods. "Tactical heave. Bring it on." He picks up his half empty bottle of beer and starts drinking again, barely even slowed down by his throwing up. He spots me sitting at the table with the shots in front of me. "Wait. You played?"

"No," I say shaking my head. "The reigning champ here was afraid to take me on. So, I thought I'd just down the shots." I didn't wait for Sebastian's reply. I pick the first shot up and down it. The Tequila tastes pretty awful, bitter, but I swallow fast and feel the warmth as it spreads through me. I chase it down with the next one and the next one until I've drained all five. I smile up at the others.

They are watching me in a state of shock.

"What?" I ask.

Rick laughs. "You didn't even flinch."

"You said you couldn't drink shots," Mark adds. "But seriously, you're on fire."

I correct him. "I said I don't drink shots. Not that I *couldn't*." Considering how little I go out, I actually have a surprisingly high tolerance for alcohol, I just don't like drinking shots. It seems so frat boy. Immature and not my style at all.

"Chance's way too grown up for shots." Sebastian chuckles. "He'd much rather have a good glass of red wine."

Actually, I'd rather have a good glass of rum or brandy, but he's not completely wrong.

"Yeah, a stag night is kind of wasted on Chance," Matt agrees.

"You don't say," I agree. "I did say I would be perfectly happy not to come."

"Don't start with that shit again." Sebastian laughs. "We're family. That means you have to show up."

"I did show up," I remind him. "But you can't pull the family card. You let Dad off the hook."

"Well yeah, because he's Dad," Sebastian replies. "You really think he'd follow the *what happens in Vegas stays in Vegas* rule? He'd spend the next lord knows how long reminding us of every stupid thing we say and do tonight."

"True," I say.

"Anyway, Vegas is hardly Dad's scene is it?" he adds.

"It's hardly my scene either," I say.

"Yeah, but you only think you're ancient and past it. You're twenty-four, start acting it." Matt laughs.

I snap. "Just because I'm the youngest, doesn't mean I have to be the dumbest." I realize I've made everyone feel awkward as I snap at Matt. "You know being the dumbest is Sebastian's thing. This is his night, so let's not try to take his title," I say with a grin, quickly turning the mood back around to laughter.

"You haven't seen anything yet. Wait until we hit the strip tonight and you'll see just how dumb I can be," Sebastian agrees.

This gets another round of cheers and another cry for shots.

I resist the urge to roll my eyes, reminding myself this is Sebastian's night not mine, and when a shot of something neon blue is handed to me, I don't resist. I tell myself I can do this. I can be the fun one for a few days. God, people do much worse things for much longer periods of time. Going to

Vegas for a few days partying is most people's idea of fun and here I am on a private jet going to stay in a nice hotel and I'm acting like I'm on death row or something.

We down the shots and the conversation moves on to the night's plans. And they say I'm the boring one. Who plans a night in Vegas? You leave your hotel, follow the lights and go with the flow. That's really what Vegas is about. Living in the moment. Being a bit reckless and doing something you wouldn't normally do.

My work phone vibrates in my pocket and I move away from the group to go back to my seat, pulling it out. I glance at the screen and roll my eyes. It's Dennis Rogers. I'm doing a full redesign for his holiday home. The plans are all done and he doesn't want the work to start until the back end of next week, and yet he's never off the phone with me. I debate ignoring his call, but I know if I do, I'll only spend the rest of this week thinking about what he wants until I call him back on Monday. I take the call.

"Mr. Rogers. Is everything okay?" I ask.

"It's Dennis," he reminds me. "And yes, everything's fine. Or at least I hope it is. I got a call from a contractor this morning about them wanting to be in the house next Wednesday afternoon. I'm not leaving until Thursday morning and I've told them that won't work, but they said they had your permission?"

"Yes. It's just what we discussed. They won't be starting any of the work. They just want to come out, get the keys from you and have you show them how the security system works. Remember? You said Wednesday would be the best day for you?"

"Oh. Yes, of course. I remember now. Sorry to have bothered you," he says.

"It's fine, really, you haven't bothered me," I lie.

"Oh. There's just one more thing," he says.

"Go on," I say through gritted teeth. Before he can respond, my phone is being snatched away from my ear.

Sebastian grins down at me with my phone in his hand.

I glare at him.

He ignores me as he looks at my phone and then puts it to his ear. "Hi, Mr. Rogers. This is Sebastian Hunter. Chance is actually taking the rest of this week off for a family thing, and he'll call you on Monday." He ends the call.

"What the fuck? That was a client," I snap, angry now.

"I know. Mr. Rogers. And you can tell him on Monday what an asshole I am. But for now, you can forget about him, forget about work, and have a good time. You were doing so well there for a moment."

I roll my eyes and hold my hand out for the phone.

Sebastian holds it out of my reach, mocking me. "Seriously Chance, you promised you wouldn't be working through my stag night."

I continue to glare at him but it has no effect on him whatsoever. I sigh. "I told you I wouldn't work while we're in Vegas. And we're not in Vegas yet."

"That's a technicality and you know it," Sebastian counters.

His little game is starting to piss me off now. Of course, I want him to enjoy his stag night but I honestly think he can have just as good a time if I take a phone call. He'd probably have had a better time if he'd just listened to my protests and let me sit this one out.

I snatch for my phone but Sebastian sees me coming and whips it back out of my reach. He throws it to Matt who catches it with one hand and promptly dumps it in a pitcher of water.

"For fuck sake!" I snap. "Have you two got no sense between you or what?"

Matt just laughs. "It's only your work phone," he points out. He peers down at the water. "It's not even your current one. Just have one weekend where you're not working. Is that really too much to ask?"

It probably isn't. It definitely isn't. But the point Matt and Sebastian are missing is that I want to work. I'm not doing it because I think the world will stop turning if I take a couple of days off. I'm doing it because I enjoy it. I like to be kept in the loop. Trying to explain this in a way that doesn't make me sound like I've lost the plot, isn't going to be easy though and I just shrug. "Fine. Whatever. You've made the decision for me now, haven't you?" I get up and turn towards the bathroom.

"Chance, wait," Sebastian says.

I turn around, stupidly thinking he's going to apologize, but then I see he's grinning.

"Matt said that's not your current work phone. Hand it over." He holds his hand out.

"So, you can put it in a jug of water? I don't think so," I reply.

"I swear I won't," he says. "I'll put it somewhere safe until after the weekend." His hand is still out and he's blocking my path.

I know it's going to be pointless to argue with him, so I take my other phone out of my pocket and slam it into his hand.

He pockets it and keeps his hand out, raising an eyebrow at me.

I sigh and pull out the third and final phone and give him that too. "If you think you're getting my personal phone, then you're very wrong," I say.

He grins and shakes his head. "Nah, you can keep that one. It's not like you have a hip and happening social life, where you'll be getting calls on that one is it?" He laughs.

I shake my head in annoyance and storm away from Sebastian and his stupid taunts. I lock myself in the bathroom, put the toilet lid down and sit on it for a moment. God, why can't I just be normal and enjoy a boozy weekend with the guys?

I stand up and wash my hands in cool water. I tell myself that's exactly what I'm going to do. Right after I get to the hotel, sort Mr. Rogers' problem out and deal with a couple of other things.

Chapter Two

CHANCE

When we arrive at our hotel, we agree to all go up to our rooms, freshen up and meet back in the lobby in two hours. Two hours sounds like an awfully long time to me and I think Sebastian secretly wants to take a nap before we head out, but I bite my tongue. It will give me time to get things in order and make a few calls from my room before we go out. And then I can keep my promise to Sebastian and stop working.

If he hadn't acted like an ass on the plane and took my phones away my work would be done now, but then lord knows, how I would have filled the next two hours.

My room is on the eleventh floor and I step out of the elevator into a nice, clean looking hallway. The walls are painted off white and the flooring is a thick red carpet. Gold light fixtures are set at even spaces along the way. The gold is a little gaudy in my opinion, but hey, it's Vegas and that's Vegas isn't it? Over the top, gaudy, cheesy. But a good night out.

I reach my room and step in. The room itself is nice and elegant looking. A large bed with a pristine white duvet takes center stage in the room. A black runner sits about three quarters of the way down it. There's a black leather sofa beneath the window with a small table beside it. The wardrobe is a built in one with mirrored doors, and there's a pine chest of drawers and bedside cabinets. Opposite the bed is a large desk with a TV on one end and space to work at the other. I grin to myself when I spot the phone. That will stop me from having to use my personal phone and risk clients getting my personal phone number.

I peer into the bathroom which is all tiled in white with the occasional black one scattered in that breaks up the white and stops the room from looking too clinical while maintaining the clean, pristine look they'd been going for. There's a large double shower and a Jacuzzi bath, both of which look shiny and clean.

As rooms go as opposed to suites, I've stayed in much worse. I open up my suitcase and quickly unpack my stuff. I find a pair of fluffy white robes hanging in the wardrobe. When I've finished unpacking, which takes less than ten minutes, I go into the bathroom and strip my suit off. It feels good to finally lose the suit as it's so hot out here. I take a shower and go back to my main room.

I get dressed for tonight in a pair of black ripped jeans and a pale blue t-shirt. I run my hands through my hair, mussing it up a little and add a spritz of Armani and I'm done. A full thirty minutes after arriving at the hotel.

I go to the mini bar and grab a rum. I add a couple of ice cubes and take it to the little table beside the leather sofa. I pick the phone up and move it to the small table. The cable just reaches and I grin to myself. Something had to go right for me work wise.

Before I begin working, I sit down and sip my rum, looking out of the window. I have a fantastic view of the strip and even though it's barely started to get dark, lights flash everywhere. It really is the perfect place for a stag night and as I sip my drink, I promise myself that once we get out tonight, I will forget about work altogether.

The decision made, I pick the receiver up, dial nine for an outside line, and call the office. I get the phone numbers I need and program them into my personal phone when I realize I don't have anything to write them on.

I call Dennis Rogers back first.

"Chance?" he says, surprised when I tell him it's me. "Your brother said you were taking the weekend off."

"Please excuse Sebastian," I say with a laugh. "It's his stag party and he's a little out of control."

"You're at his stag party and you're working? Seriously, this can wait until Monday. Have a great time and have a drink or two for me." He ends the call before I can argue with him.

I frown a little. Even my clients are telling me to ignore work for a few days. If only it was that simple. I shake my head and smile to myself. If I'd spent my time slacking off, partying and dating, then I wouldn't be where I am now. I joined the firm straight out of college and I've worked my ass off ever since to prove that I'm the best at what I do in the city.

I think I've proved that. My clients always come back to me, and my services are booked in advance for the next year. I know deep down I have nothing else to prove and I know if I took a step back, the talented designers who work alongside me would be able to do a great job, but it's just not me. Why would I have worked so hard to get to where I am if I just wanted to slack off and hand my work off to others? If that's all I'd wanted to do, I could have taken a more corporate role but the thought fills me with horror. Being stuck in an office all day and never getting to do anything creative is my idea of hell.

I make a few more calls and then I check the time. I have about twenty minutes before I have to meet the others and I pick the phone back up to make one more call. I listen to it ringing and then a female voice asks how she can direct my call. I give her my name and the name of my client and she asks me to hold for a moment. Dreadful hold music fills my ears.

My hotel room door bursts open and I glance up in annoyance as Sebastian comes bounding in, calling my name. I cover the mouthpiece of the phone in case my call goes through and hiss at Sebastian to shut up.

He just laughs. He comes further into the room and shakes his head when he sees me on a call. He marches to the desk and bends down. He sticks his hand behind the desk and the line goes dead in my ear. Sebastian straightens back up and grins at me, showing me the cord he's just disconnected from the socket.

I slam the receiver down and get to my feet. I'm taller than Sebastian and I stand over him, glaring at him in frustration and anger. "What the fuck are you playing at Sebastian?" I demand as I step closer to him, my anger showing.

Sebastian ducks out of my way, but he's still laughing and waving the cord, taunting me. It's like he wants me to punch him or something. "Relax Chance. You're more uptight than Dad. I know you think Kimberley and I won't last, but I'm telling you, she's the one, and—"

"What makes you think I think you and Kimberley won't last?" I interrupt him.

"Because I've spent so long playing the field," he says.

"Only because you were trying to get over her in the first place," I say. I know that's not the real reason he thinks that. I can see it on his face. I rack my brains, trying to think of anytime I've said something that he could have taken to mean I thought him and Kimberley were doomed. I can't think of anything. "Come on Seb. Why do you really think that?"

"Well, the whole love and marriage thing isn't really your thing is it?" he says.

"Not at all," I agree. "But that doesn't mean I think it's not for everyone. You and Kimberley are made for each other."

"So, why aren't you taking this seriously then?" Sebastian demands. "I'm only ever going to have one stag party and you can't stop working two fucking days for it?"

Maybe, he has a point. Yeah, he does. But that doesn't excuse him cutting off one of my calls not once, but twice today. He had no idea who those calls were to, and even once he saw my client's name on the screen on the plane, he had no idea how he would react to being essentially told to fuck off. He could have cost the firm a lot of business.

"Fine. I'll stop," I say.

"Good." He grins then shakes his head. "I honestly can't believe we're in Vegas and I'm having to impose a no working rule. The hard part should be convincing everyone it's over and they have to go back to work."

"Whatever. I've told you I'll stop. Now, do me a favor, and stay the hell out of my room, otherwise you're not going to live long enough to marry Kimberley."

"Ooh, fightin' words." Sebastian grins. "Bring it on, bro." He's dancing around the room, his fists up.

I try to stay mad at him, but I'm laughing at his antics.

"Ah see, you can smile without your face breaking," he teases me and stops dancing around. "We're going to have a couple in the hotel bar before we head out. Are you ready?"

Before I can answer, Matt steps into the room. "Why is Sierra downstairs in reception?" he asks me.

Fucking hell. This is just getting worse. She was meant to sneak in without either of my brothers or Bradley seeing her.

Both Matt and Sebastian are staring at me now, their eyes burning a hole into my guilty face, waiting for an explanation.

"Look, I agreed not to work for this weekend. But that doesn't mean shit can just be left to not get done. Sierra will be taking care of a few things for me while we're here, that's all," I say.

"It takes your work obsession to a whole new level when you can't go on a stag night without bringing your assistant along." Matt smirks.

"I'm glad you think this is funny," Sebastian says. "Do you have any idea how much trouble I'm going to be in now?"

I narrow my eyes at him. "You think Kimberley will be jealous because Sierra's here?" I ask.

He laughs and shakes his head. "God, no. But Bernie will. She's pretty much my best friend and I told her she couldn't come out here with us because it's a guy thing. She got it, but it'll be a whole different ball game if she finds out about this."

"It's not like she's here for the party," I defend. "And besides, hen parties are always rowdier than stag parties. She'll have a much better time with the girls."

He shrugs. "Just make sure you tell her I had no idea about this if she finds out," Sebastian says.

"I will. I'd better go and find Sierra and see what's taking her so long. I just have to quickly go through what I need her to focus on and I'll meet you two in the bar in ten." I grab my room key, phone and wallet and leave the room, reminding them to flick the lock over when they leave. I walk away knowing they're both staring after me.

I head down to the lobby, quietly fuming. I'm annoyed at my brothers; they don't want to work this week, yet they don't seem to want anyone else covering the work that needs to be done either. I'm still annoyed at Sierra too. I mean how hard is it to be in a place the size of fucking Vegas and not get seen by the few people who would recognize you?

I step out of the elevator and cross the lobby.

Sierra is just turning away from the check-in desk. She's wearing a sensible knee length pencil skirt with a white blouse and a black jacket. If she's too hot, she's not showing it. Her ashy blonde hair is clipped up in a French pleat. She clacks across the lobby in her heels.

"Sierra," I shout.

She turns to face me. Her perfect posture doesn't falter, but she gives her nerves away by pushing her glasses up. Something she always does when she's nervous. She comes to stand before me. "I'm so sorry Mr. Hunter," she says. "I checked the lobby before I came in, but then there was a problem at the desk and it took longer to sort it out than I thought it would, and then Matt was there. I tried to lie to him, but he saw straight through it. Have I caused a whole lot of trouble?"

I can feel some of the anger leaving me. Sierra has been my assistant for the last two years, and this is the only mistake I can ever remember her making. If this is as bad as it gets, then we're all good.

I shake my head. "No, I'll handle it. Now what was the problem at reception?" I ask.

"They said they couldn't find a room booked for me. I had to beg them to let me go up to your room and find out what was going on. They only agreed because I showed them my company ID and they recognized your name," she says.

"Wait here. I'll fix it," I say. I go up to the desk and flash a smile at the receptionist there. "My name's Chance Hunter. I have two adjacent rooms booked for this evening and tomorrow evening. My assistant has just tried to check into hers and she was told there's no record of her having a room booked here."

"Let me check that for you, sir. Chance Hunter you said?"

I nod.

She starts clicking on her keyboard. She gives me a professional smile. "I see the booking here." She makes another few clicks. "Oh, I see the problem. Because you had already checked in when your assistant arrived, the booking moved to another part of the system. I'm sorry. My colleague is new and wouldn't have known to check there."

"No worries," I say.

She hands me a key card and wishes me a pleasant stay.

If only she knew. I turn back to Sierra.

Rick is talking to her and as I get closer, I hear their conversation.

"So yeah. I'm in room 217 if you want some company later," Rick says.

I see Sierra tense up as she shakes her head. "As I said, I'm here for work. And I don't know if that line has ever worked for you before, but I can assure you it wouldn't work on me even if I was here for pleasure."

I shake my head and shove Rick away from her.

He frowns at me. "What? I can't talk to women now?"

"You can talk to women all you want, just quit harassing this one. This is Sierra, my assistant," I say.

"Oh. Sorry," he says. He winks at Sierra. "You can't blame a guy for trying, can you?"

She smiles and shakes her head.

Rick wanders over to join Mark.

"Sorry about that." I hand her the key for her room. "Your room is 1124. It's next door to mine, so if you need anything, you know where to find me. Did you bring the Bramer files like I asked?"

She nods her head.

"Good," I say. "He has some rather bizarre requests as you'll see. It could take weeks to source some of that stuff, so if you can make a start on going through it all, that would be great. I also need you to arrange a meeting with Vince Falcrow. Oh, and can you send Dennis Rogers something. An apology for Sebastian cutting off our call earlier. I've spoken to him since and he's fine about it, but it won't hurt."

"Got it," Sierra says. "And what do you want me to do about Millicent Burroughs? She's been calling non-stop since you pushed her meeting back."

"I'll get back to you on that one," I say. *When I remember who the hell she is*, I don't add.

"Okay, well if that's it then, I'll go and make a start," Sierra says.

"Wait," Rick says.

I hadn't noticed him sidling back over.

"Seriously, Chance? You've dragged the poor woman all the way out here and you're not even letting her take a night to herself to see the sights?" he asks.

"And that's your business because?" I ask.

He shrugs and wanders back away again.

He makes it sound like slave labor. I mean it's not like I've dragged Sierra out here against her will and her bonus will more than make up for any inconvenience. But he does have a point though. I mean it is Vegas. I smile at Sierra. "He's right," I say. "Take the night off and take in the sights. There's plenty of time tomorrow for work."

"Thank you Mr. Hunter," she says with a smile.

I return her smile and go to find the others in the bar.

Chapter Three

SIERRA

As I head up to my room, I find that I can't get Chance out of my head. He looked so different in his jeans and t-shirt. Trendy. It's funny because he's two years younger than me, but I always think of him as older. Out of the three Hunter brothers, if I didn't know them, I would say Chance was the oldest. There's a maturity about him and he's always so well presented. But tonight he looked... different.

Don't get me wrong. I've always thought he was good looking. He has a strong jaw, full lips and beautiful blue eyes. His fair hair is always just the right amount of mussed up and he's tall and muscular. But I've never looked at him and felt myself respond to his looks like I did tonight.

Not that it matters. I mean nothing can ever happen between us. Chance is my boss and I'm not someone who acts unprofessional. Plus, he's a total workaholic and I could never be with someone who didn't have time for our relationship.

Our relationship. God, listen to me. You'd think he'd asked me out or something. All he did was give me a night off, and it's a night I would normally have had off anyway. I shake my head, pushing away my silly daydreams as I step out of the elevator and go to find my room.

I find it easily and step inside. It's nice, better than nice, luxurious. I knew it would be though. Chance had never been one to stay somewhere nice and put me somewhere cheap when we've been to conferences and stuff.

I unpack my things and take my suit off. I look at the clothes I've brought, wondering what to wear now I've got the night off. I settle on a knee length black dress and heels. I get dressed and look at myself in the mirror.

I sit down on the end of the bed. I really do want to go out and explore Vegas, but where would I go on my own? I'm kind of hungry, but sitting alone in a restaurant in Vegas is just too pathetic for words.

I decide to go for a walk along the strip and go to one of the casinos. Loads of people go to those alone, so I won't look out of place. And then I'll grab some takeout food to bring back up to my room once I'm done.

I'm humming to myself as I grab my bag and head for the door. I place my hand on the handle and a loud knock sounds from the other side. I make a startled yelping sound and then I tell myself not to be paranoid.

I open the door and my heart sinks when I see Chance standing there. I guess a night off was too much to ask for after all. It looks like it's going to be a slice of pizza while I work tonight.

Chapter Four

CHANCE

I wake up slowly and the first thing, no, the only thing, I notice is the absolute fucking blinding pain in my head. The light streaming in the window is dazzling me and I close my eyes, trying to drift off to sleep again, but it's no use. There's no way I will be able to get to sleep with my head pounding like this. I sit up slowly, the room spinning around me. I kick my feet over the side of the bed and groan quietly.

What the fuck happened last night? Clearly, I drank far too much, but right now, it feels more like I was run over about fifty times. I blink a few times and the spinning stops. I run my hands over my face and groan again, louder this time.

A gasp from behind me startles me to my feet.

Sierra sits up, pulling the sheet up to cover her naked breasts. *Her naked breasts. What the fuck?* Even through the pain in my head and my utter confusion I can't help but notice her eyes. Without her glasses hiding them, they sparkle brightly. Even with the mascara smudges beneath them and the creases in her face from the pillow, I notice how beautiful she is. Her hair hangs around her face and over her shoulders. It's so much longer than I imagined it. It's got a slight curl to it that suits her.

"Mr. Hunter," she says, not looking at me. "What's going on?"

I think we're well past her calling me Mr. Hunter, but I don't say that. Instead, I just gape at her like an idiot for a few moments.

Her eyes flit to my face and then she looks away again.

"I-I don't know," I admit. I clear my throat awkwardly. *What the hell happened between us? Why is Sierra in my bed? And why is someone inside of my head banging away with a huge hammer?*

"Why do you keep looking at me like that?" Sierra asks quietly.

Because you're absolutely stunning and I've never noticed it before and I can't understand how I've never seen it. "I guess I'm just not used to seeing you with your hair down," I say.

I mean it literally. I've never seen Sierra without a French pleat or a tight bun in her hair.

She raises an eyebrow and looks at me, keeping her eyes firmly on my face. She gives me a half smile. "I could say the same about you," she says.

I frown, confused, and her eyes flicker down for just a second. Long enough for me to realize I am standing there completely naked, my morning wood pointing at Sierra like an accusatory finger. "Shit, sorry." I spot my boxer shorts on the ground and I grab them and pull them on.

"I feel like I've been hit by a train," Sierra says, rubbing her temples.

"Yeah. I know that feeling," I say.

"Can I use your bathroom?" she asks.

I nod.

She pulls the sheet tighter around herself. Wrapped up in it, she heads towards the bathroom door. She goes inside and closes the door.

I am still in a state of total and utter confusion, but I know I can't still be as good as naked when she comes back out, and I start to gather up my clothes.

My clothes aren't in the neat pile I would normally leave them in. They're scattered all over. That could mean one of two things though. It could mean that Sierra and I were in the throes of passion and stripping off as we moved towards the bed. Or it could mean that I was blind drunk and was just taking my clothes off at random as I moved through the room, ready to collapse into bed.

Surely, it has to be option two. That would make the most sense. I can't work out why Sierra is here though. I decide to just stop thinking about it for a moment. It's not making anything any clearer and my head is hurting worse the more I try to make sense of anything.

I pull my jeans on with a sigh. I fasten the button and as I'm pulling the zip up, a scream comes from the bathroom. I run towards the door, calling out to make sure Sierra is okay.

Chapter Five

SIERRA

I sit down on the closed lid of the toilet, the sheet still gathered around me. My head is fuzzy, aching and I feel kind of nauseous. I can live with that though. It's only a hangover; nothing a few aspirin won't cure. The aspirin won't bring my memory back though.

What the actual fuck did I drink last night that was so potent that I have no recollection of the night before? I mean I've woken up a little disoriented before, but never in someone else's bed without knowing how I got there. And I've always been able to piece the night together after a couple of minutes.

Think Sierra I tell myself. I can't though. It's just a blank space in my head where last night should be. I can't help but think of Chance. An image flashes through my head of him standing beside the bed, his cock on show. I can't help but smile despite myself. Chance is always so together, not someone who gets rattled. But his face when he realized his cock was not only out, but was hard and pointing in my direction. If I hadn't been so embarrassed, I probably would have laughed right there and then.

I've known Chance for two years, and I've never seen him at a loss for words. He's usually so articulate. He's not a babbler, but he always knows the right thing to say for any occasion. But apparently, this morning threw him as much as it threw me, because he just stood there, his mouth opening and closing with no sound coming out.

I know we didn't have sex. Well, no actually, I don't know that. But I mean I don't think we did. Why would we? Neither of us have ever been anything but professional before. There's been no flirting, no suggestive looks. We've barely even spoken to each other except for work related things. Hell, until last night, I hadn't even seen him in casual clothes and he'd never seen me with my hair down.

Well, that's certainly all changed.

I try again to remember last night. I remember checking in to the hotel and Chance giving me the night off. So I must have left my room and went for a drink somewhere. That much is clear by the pounding in my head. So maybe I ran into Chance and the others somewhere. I mean I wouldn't have just come to his room drunk and uninvited would I?

Oh my God, would I? Did I?

Panic fills me at the thought of a drunken me knocking on Chance's room door and slurring at him. I shake my head, pushing the image away. Even if, for whatever reason, I had done that, he hadn't exactly sent me packing had he?

"I'm never drinking again," I whisper.

I get to my feet and glance into the mirror. I gasp at the state of myself. My hair is a wavy mess and I have mascara stains underneath my eyes. My skin is a dead looking grey color. *Thanks hangover.*

I can't change whatever happened last night, but I can control what happens next, at least to an extent. I can freshen up a bit and not go out there looking like I've rolled in straight out of the trash.

I turn the cold tap on, clutching the sheet with one hand. I wet the other hand and run it over my hair, taming the worst of the wavy bits. *Oh, who am I kidding?* They're not wavy bits. They're frizzy bits. I rub at the mascara underneath my eyes. I manage to get the most of it off.

I tuck the sheet in on itself, so both of my hands are free as I cup water into my hands and splash it onto my face. I'm starting to feel a little more human now. I reach out to turn the tap off and a flash of gold catches my eye.

My eyes widen and panic fills my whole body.

"No, no, no," I whisper.

I close my eyes shut. I'm imagining it. I must be. Yes, I'm still a little drunk and my mind is playing tricks on me. When I open my eyes again, it'll be gone and I'll be able to laugh at my huge overreaction to something I imagined. It was just a trick of the light. Nothing more.

I count to three in my head and I open my eyes.

It's still there and before I can stop myself, I let out a scream. I cut the scream off and hold my breath, praying Chance didn't hear me.

"Sierra? Are you alright in there?" Chances shouts, tapping on the door.

Okay, he heard me. Of course he heard me. He's not deaf or fucking dead. Half of the hotel probably heard me.

I move towards the door. I might as well just tell him now. I'm going to have to tell him at some point. Maybe he remembers a little more than I do and he knows where it came from.

"Sierra?" Chance calls again.

I pull the bathroom door open.

"Are you okay? I heard you scream. What happened?"

I try to find the words to tell him, but they just don't come. I stand while staring mutely at him for a moment.

He stares back at me with a look of concern.

Great. Now, he thinks I've lost my mind.

I give up trying to find the words to explain why I screamed, and instead, I hold up my left hand, trying not to look at the offending gold band on my wedding finger.

Chance stares at my hand, his concern giving way to a frown of confusion. "I don't see anything Sierra. Did you hurt your hand or something?"

I wish that was all it was. I wish I'd slipped over on the floor and broke my wrist or something. Six weeks in a cast and it's all good. Just another dumb Vegas accident. But the dumb Vegas accident I seem to have had is so much worse than that. "The wedding ring," I manage to say. "Mr. Hunter, I'm not married, or at least I wasn't. And I wasn't wearing this ring yesterday."

His face pales as the realization of what I'm saying dawns on him. In slow motion, he lifts his left hand and we both look at it at the same moment.

"Oh fuck," we both say together when we see the matching gold band on his finger.

Chapter Six

CHANCE

I am backing away from Sierra as the realization of what happened hits me. I feel the bed hit the back of my legs as I sit down hard and rub my hands over my face. I look up at Sierra.

She is still standing in the bathroom doorway staring at me.

I realize the way I've backed away from her wasn't exactly tactful and I shake my head a little trying to clear it. "I'm sorry Sierra," I say. "I'm just trying to make sense of all of this and well, it's not really happening."

She gives a soft laugh. "Yeah. Tell me about it. Mr. Hunter I don't mean to be rude, but do you think you could hand me my clothes? And then we can talk." she says.

"You know what? Why don't I go downstairs and get us some coffee? You can get dressed in peace and maybe the caffeine will clear our minds a little," I say.

"That would be great," she says.

I pick up my t-shirt from the bed behind me and pull it on. I get up and head for the door. "Oh and Sierra? I think we're way past formalities. Just call me Chance."

I've been telling her that since pretty much the moment she joined the company, but she's always insisted it's not professional to call her boss by his first name. Surely, now she'll start though. I mean who calls their husband by his full title? I pause and wonder why I just thought this in such a casual way. Her husband?

I head downstairs to the bar. It's only when I get there I realize I have no idea how Sierra takes her coffee. I've worked with her for two years and I don't even know whether she takes milk and sugar in her coffee. That's pretty bad.

I order a latte for me and an Americano for Sierra. I grab a couple of packs of sugar and a couple of little milk cartons. There. She can make it how she likes it. I head back up to my room.

As I walk along the corridor, a thought occurs to me. If neither of us really knows what happened last night, how do we even know we're married? No I tell myself, we have to be. It's way too much of a coincidence for both of us to have gone out, gotten drunk and then married total strangers. Not that Sierra isn't a total stranger to me even though technically, I know her. I make a note to myself to take an interest in getting to know my employees more. I mean look at Sebastian. His assistant knows more about him than anyone, and he knows as much about her. I bet he knows how she takes her coffee.

It has to be Sierra that I got married to. I mean how else would we have ended up in bed together? I wonder fleetingly again what we did in bed, if we consummated the marriage, but that's hardly what I should be focusing on right now.

I get back to my room and I reach out to let myself in, but then I let my hand fall away. What if Sierra is naked in there? Suddenly awkward, I knock on the door. I hear a gasp come from inside and I smile to myself. Sierra doesn't know it's me. She's probably trying to work out how she would explain herself being in there in a state of undress if it's one of my brothers at the door.

"It's me," I call.

She whips the door open.

I step inside.

She's back in her dress from last night and she looks a bit more composed. Certainly more composed than I feel.

"I didn't know how you take it," I say as I hand her the coffee, the milks and sugar.

"Black with two sugars," she smiles as she tears open a sugar packet. "I hate to break it to you, but what you drink isn't coffee. It's warm milk with a bit of flavoring."

I smile at her and shake my head. "And what you drink is just sweet water," I grin.

She finishes putting the sugar in her coffee and then she sits down on the edge of the bed. She takes a sip and winces when it burns her lip, but the heat doesn't stop her going back for another sip. "That's better." She smiles. "I don't understand these people that can face the day without coffee."

"Me neither." I sit down beside her on the bed and start working on my own coffee. It numbs the dull ache in my head a little. "So do you remember anything from last night?" I ask. "Tell me everything you remember, no matter how trivial it seems. We might be able to trigger each other's memories a bit."

"I remember checking in," she says. "And you giving me the night off. I came up to my room, unpacked and got changed. I decided to go down the strip and visit one of the casinos." She pauses and then she gasps. "Wait! I remember something. I was just about to leave. I picked my bag up. And then there was a knock on my room door. It was you. You said I should join you all, because being in Vegas alone was no fun."

Her words spark a memory in me and I find myself nodding along. "Yes. That's right. Rick, the guy who was hitting on you at check in? He told the others that I gave you the night off, and Matt said I should have invited you out with us. The others joined in, so I started to feel bad. I said I'd come up and see if you wanted to come for a few drinks. Sebastian told me to tell you not to tell Bernie, because she'd be mad if she found out you'd come along when he'd told her it was guys only."

She laughs softly. "Well, you can tell him his secrets are safe with me. I can't tell Bernie something I don't remember. Even if I wanted to."

I don't know if it's talking about the bits we remember of the night, or whether the coffee is finally having an effect on me, but my mind is starting to clear a little bit and I'm remembering more. "Wait, we had dinner. All of us. We went to a high end restaurant and you said it was a rip off and we should have just gone to McDonalds. I told you the food was better quality and you laughed and said it's Vegas – it's all crap aimed at tourists, and we did it, didn't we? We all went to McDonalds."

"Yes!" Sierra exclaims. "We got cheeseburgers and milkshakes. We must have already been drunk at that point though."

"How do you know?"

"Because we didn't go to McDonalds because any of you believed me about the restaurant being a tourist trap. We ended up there because the restaurant told us we were too loud and Sebastian got into an argument with the waiter. Matt said we should leave because he wasn't going to be the one to tell Kimberley why Sebastian had a black eye or something at their wedding."

"Right, so it must have been quite late when we went for food then. I remember us drinking in the hotel bar. I think we ended up staying here later than we planned. And I vaguely remember us going to a casino and playing blackjack."

Sierra stands up and goes and gets her handbag. She opens it, peers in and laughs. "Yup. I still have chips in my bag," she says. "Wait. I have a receipt here as well." She studies the receipt for a moment and then her cheeks go pink.

"What is it?" I ask.

She doesn't speak, she just hands me the slip of paper.

It's a ticket for entry to what I assume is a bar. It's called The Curious Cat.

"Why are you blushing?" I ask. "What is this place? It's just a bar isn't it?"

"Not exactly," she says. "It's a strip club."

I feel myself blushing as well. I mean it's a stag night. It was going to happen. But when I pictured us going to a strip club, I didn't picture Sierra being with us.

"What happens in Vegas stays in Vegas right?" She smiles.

I nod. *Damn right. Except I can't really leave my actual fucking wife behind.*

"Is there a time on it?" Sierra asks.

I check the receipt again and nod. "Yeah. According to this, we went there at 10.17," I say.

"So it wasn't that late then and we must have already been smashed. Otherwise, I don't think you'd have been up for taking your assistant to a strip club." Sierra laughs as she says it, blushing again.

The blush suits her. It makes her look sweet and innocent, like she needs looking after and protecting from the seedier side of the world. I shake my head. *Where the hell did that come from?*

"And that's it," Sierra says. "After that, it's all just a total blur."

I nod in agreement. "I remember us drinking some vile pink concoction in the strip club, but I don't remember much else about being there. Or what happened after."

We go quiet for a moment, both of us wracking our brains, trying to bring the rest of the night back to our memories. I sigh after a few minutes. It's hopeless. Even the parts that have come back to me are patchy at best, and they're in no logical order.

There's one thought that keeps coming back to me though; the elephant in the room, and I decide to just say it, "Sierra, we can't stay married. It's just a ridiculous mistake that we have to fix." I don't want to hurt her, but God, we can't stay married.

Sierra looks at me for a minute. Her bottom lip is quivering.

Oh God, she's going to cry. How the hell am I meant to fix this without Sierra ending up feeling used or hating me?

Sierra bursts into laughter.

I relax a little. I don't know what I've said that's so funny, but at least her lip wasn't wobbling because she was upset. She was trying to hold back her laughter rather than tears.

"No shit Sherlock!" she says through her laughter.

My jaw drops open. She's never said anything like that to me before, but then again, she's never been my wife before. The ridiculousness of the situation hits me and I find myself laughing with her.

After a couple of minutes, Sierra gets herself back under control. She wipes tears of laughter from her cheeks. "I'm sorry Mr. Hunter. I didn't mean to say that. But oh my God, your face. You were looking at me like you were worried I was going to pitch a fit and demand we stay married."

I can't help but laugh. "Sorry. I just—I have no idea how to handle this situation. And it's Chance."

"Yeah, me neither. It's not something you encounter every day is it? I thought the whole Vegas wedding thing only happened in really bad movies."

"Yeah. The ones everyone eye rolls at because it's ridiculous that two normal people could find themselves in that situation," I agree.

"Exactly," Sierra agrees. "But just to put your mind at rest, I agree that we have to find a way out of this. Of course, it was a mistake. You know, I'm starting to think they pump something into the air in this place."

"Maybe they do." I nod. "It would explain a lot wouldn't it? And it's a much better story than we got blind drunk and thought why not?"

"Definitely," Sierra says. "So I think the easiest way to deal with this will be to get the marriage annulled Mr. Hun—Chance. It feels so weird calling you Chance."

"Weirder than being married to me?" I grin.

"Maybe not that weird." She smiles. "So any idea how to get a marriage annulled?"

"Nope." I shrug.

"Me either," she says. "But I do know my way around Google better than anyone. Give me an hour to shower and change. Then find out what we need to do and I'll come back to you."

"Sounds like a plan," I say.

Chapter Seven

CHANCE

I wait until Sierra leaves. Then I go shower and get changed myself. The pain in my head is almost gone, but my memory doesn't seem to be working any better. Maybe it's better I don't remember. I mean at this point, what could remembering the whole night do except make this whole situation even more cringey and awkward?

Exactly an hour later, there's a knock at my door. I can't help but smile to myself at Sierra's punctual arrival. I wonder if she's been standing in the corridor looking at her watch, waiting for the exact right second to knock.

I go and open the door and she comes in.

She's wearing a pair of black trousers and a pale pink button up shirt. Her hair is back up in its French pleat and any sign of the softness I saw on her face this morning when she'd just woken up is gone. Sierra is well and truly back in work mode.

"Okay," she says, all business. "So the process of annulment is pretty simple. One of us needs to file for the annulment. I'll do it on the grounds that I was intoxicated. I know we both were, but Nevada state law only permits one person to file the request. Filing the request can be done online and I've already found a notary willing to witness it. After that, the court will attempt to contact you to notify you of the claim. Don't respond and after twenty days, I can then request the court make a decision based on the fact you're not responding. Hopefully, then, they grant the annulment."

"Wouldn't it be quicker if I responded?" I ask.

Sierra shrugs. "Maybe. But then we'd have to go to court. This way, it can all be done behind closed doors."

"Okay, that makes sense," I say.

"There's just one catch," she adds. "Before I can file the complaint, we need a witness who can verify that I was intoxicated at the time of the marriage."

"Oh, shit," I say. "That complicates things doesn't it?"

"It does. But someone must have acted as the witness to our wedding. If we can track them down, they might be able to help us out."

"So we need to know where we got married then," I say.

She nods.

I grab my laptop and sit down on the bed and fire it up.

"I've already Googled it. There are thousands of places we could have gotten married," she says.

"But there can't be that many within walking distance of The Curious Cat," I conclude. "I know we could have gotten a cab from there and ended up anywhere in the city, but we might as well start there."

She frowns a little and then nods. "Good idea."

"You say that like you're surprised." I laugh. "Like maybe you think I'm all beauty and no brains. And before you say anything about not thinking I'm beautiful, just remember you married me."

She laughs again and her face softens, her eyes sparkling.

I can't believe I've never noticed before, how her eyes sparkle when she laughs. She sits down beside me on the bed as my laptop fires up and I navigate to Google. I pick up the receipt from The Curious Cat from the bedside cabinet and look for the address. I find it and type it into the search bar and then I add wedding.

Within ten minutes, I have a list of twelve wedding venues within walking distance of The Curious Cat.

"Ready?" I ask.

Sierra nods and gets up.

We head downstairs and out of the hotel.

I'm glad it's still early, way too early for any of the others from our party to be up and about. I just want this thing to go away without anyone having to know about it. I'm fairly confident that only Sierra and I were present for the wedding. The others wouldn't have let us do something this stupid.

I look around, but there isn't a cab in sight. *Perfect.* "Let's just start walking and we'll flag a cab when we can," I say.

We head in what I think is the right direction.

"Thank you," I say after a couple of minutes of silence.

"For what?" she asks, looking at me with confusion.

"For making this easy. Or at least as easy as it's going to be. I know you don't want this anymore than I do. But well, there's plenty of women who would have seen an opportunity for a hefty divorce settlement rather than an annulment."

Sierra studies me for a moment. "You know I didn't think of that. So how much would a quiet divorce be worth to you?"

I look over at her in shock.

She laughs. "I'm joking. Jeez. I know you're not used to socializing, but sometimes, people make jokes, just for the sheer hell of it you know." She smiles.

"I do occasionally socialize you know," I point out.

"You just didn't think I had any personality?" she asks.

"No. I mean yes. I knew obviously you did, but well, I've never really seen it," I say.

She shrugs. "I like to stay professional. Things get messy when you mix business and pleasure."

"You don't say." I laugh.

Sierra darts away from me and sticks her hand out.

I look up and see she's spotted a cab which pulls up beside her. She gets in and slides across the seat and I get in beside her.

I pull my list out of my pocket. It could be any of them, so I just decide to start at the top. I give the driver the address and he gives me a knowing smile through his mirror before he pulls away. He knows exactly what we've done and exactly what we're doing now.

Sierra seems to have noticed too and she peers out of the window in silence.

I feel bad for her suddenly, like I want to say something to make this less awkward, but what can I say that will fix this mess?

After a few attempts to make conversation that are met with a grunt from me and total silence from Sierra, the cab driver shrugs and turns the radio on. Marvin Gaye's voice fills the cab, singing *Let's Get It On*. Of course, it does. Because why wouldn't the universe find a way to make this even more fucking awkward?

I glance at Sierra and see she's looking at me too.

"I've been trying to figure out how to say this, and there's really no way to say it right. So I'm just going to come out with it," she says.

I nod for her to go on, already guessing what she's going to ask. The perfectly timed song has obviously sent her mind to the exact same place it's sent mine. She's blushing furiously now which only makes me more sure of what she's going to ask. I want to cut her off and tell her not to say it, but maybe if we just get this part over with, the awkwardness between us will disappear.

"Did we have sex last night?" she asks, her voice barely above a whisper.

If I hadn't already known what she was going to ask, I would have had to ask her to repeat herself. *Awkward.*

I wrack my brains yet again, trying to think if we had sex or not. I mean she was in my bed and we'd just gotten married, so that sure implies we did. But then we were drunk enough to think getting married was a good idea and blank out our entire memories of the night, so maybe neither of us were up for more than a quick fumble before we fell asleep.

I try to imagine kissing Sierra, holding her. It brings back a brief flash of us laughing together. Dancing. I'm holding her tightly against me. But that's in a bar somewhere. It doesn't help me answer her question.

I realize I've been quiet too long and Sierra is waiting for an answer. I owe her a reply if nothing else. "I'm sorry. I really don't know."

"I mean I keep thinking of how we were in bed together," she speaks again. "And then the marriage thing. It makes me think we did. But I'm not in the habit of sleeping with guys after one night." She smiles a little. "Or marrying them."

I return her smile and then I shake my head. "I really am sorry about this whole mess. This whole thing, Vegas, partying, strip clubs. Whatever happened between us. It's all just... out of character for me. I—"

I stop talking when Sierra throws her head back and laughs. "I've worked for you for two years, Chance. We had to get married before I even felt comfortable using your first name because you're so—so professional and detached. You don't have to tell me this is out of character for you. No one knows that better than I do."

I smile. Sierra is right. She knows this isn't me, and there's no way she's thinking I somehow duped her into this just to have sex with her.

"There's really no need to apologize," she goes on. "It seems we both let our guard down a little too much. And I know I can't remember most of the night, but from the bits I do remember, I feel like we had a damned good time. Whatever we did."

"Sebastian always says the best nights are the ones you can't remember." I smile.

Sierra suddenly starts to laugh again. "I keep seeing your face this morning when you saw me in your bed. And then when you realized you were naked!" Her laughter increases.

I frown. It wasn't funny. It was just embarrassing all round. But as I listen to Sierra laugh and see the tears running down her face as her laughter gets her completely, it hits me that actually, it was pretty damned funny, and before I know it, I'm laughing with her. "My head was so fuzzy and I couldn't fathom out why you wouldn't look at me." I laugh. "It just didn't even click that I was naked."

"Yeah, I figured as much by the way you reacted when you did realize. You know, I told one of my friends I was coming out to Vegas for a few days and she asked if I'd be seeing any kind of strip show. I think I can well and truly tick that one off my bucket list." She makes a tick sign in the air, still giggling.

"Yeah it puts a whole new slant on getting to know your boss a little better huh?" I grin.

"That's for sure. I mean if I'd known this was the sort of work that was going to bring me to Vegas, I'd have packed so much differently."

"Oh. And what would you have brought?" I realize, too late to stop myself from saying it, that I'm flirting with Sierra. I open my mouth to apologize, but instead of being offended or shocked, she just laughs.

She screws her face up while she thinks about it for a moment. "Fluffy handcuffs." She grins. "Much nicer underwear. But the main thing – definitely a camera."

My eyes widen.

She flushes pink and pushes her glasses up her nose, but she's still laughing. "God, I just realized how that sounded. I wasn't thinking that we should be making an amateur porn video or anything. I just wanted a picture of the look of absolute shock on your face this morning." she giggles.

"I don't think I'll need a picture to remember that." I grin. "I mean I know we seem to have forgotten a lot of last night, but this morning is firmly embedded in my mind."

"Same actually." She nods her head.

Great. Now every time my assistant looks at me, she's going to be picturing my cock pointing at her. The thought should horrify me, but instead, I find it comical and I laugh again. "So the next time I tell you to take a night off, just remind me of that moment and tell me no."

"Oh, don't worry. I'm never, ever drinking again!" She exclaims.

I want to ask her if that means nothing would ever happen between us again, or if it just means she wouldn't want to forget it if it did, but I do manage to catch myself in time to stop this time. *What sort of a question is that?* One that's guaranteed to bring this conversation full circle and all the way back to awkward, that's for sure. I am saved from trying to think up anything else to say when the cab begins to pull in beside the curb.

The cab driver turns the radio off. "Here we are," he says.

As he tells me the price, my phone begins to ring. I hand Sierra my wallet. "Can you pay for the cab while I take this please?"

She nods and I get out of the cab wondering which client has managed to get hold of my personal number and how big the problem must be for anyone at the office to give it out.

I pull my phone out and see it's not a client at all. It's Matt. I let the call ring out and go to voicemail. No one, especially not my brothers, can ever know about this, and it's better they think I'm still passed out in a drunken stupor than me trying to come up with a plausible excuse for why I'm up and about and yet, not going to meet up with them.

Sierra gets out of the cab and hands me my wallet. "Is everything okay? You look kind of nervous."

I nod my head. "I'm fine," I tell her. "It was just Matt. I let it go to voicemail."

"Yeah, heaven forbid he finds out you spent the night with the hired help," she retorts.

I don't want her to think for a second that it's like that. I am mortified about last night, but I'm not ashamed to have anyone know I was with her because I don't think she's good enough for me. I'm ashamed because I have acted so unprofessionally. "Sierra," I start.

I trail off when she looks at me. Her eyes are sparkling again, and she's trying not to laugh. Her laughter comes out when I am still staring at her and she shakes her head.

"You know, this is almost too easy." She grins.

I don't have an answer to that because she's right. She is drawing me in each and every time, and each and every time, I think she's being serious and I don't risk laughing in case I really have upset her.

She turns serious suddenly and looks at me with a vulnerable look. One I've never seen on her face before. "For what it's worth, I don't want this getting out any more than you do. Do you have any idea the kind of talk that would go around the office if people thought I was sleeping with the boss?"

"If anyone had anything to say about it, they'd have me to answer to," I growl. *Shit. Where did that come from?*

Sierra looks up at me, surprised, but I think she's a little pleased too.

We meet each other's gaze for a moment, and I feel... something. I clear my throat. "Right. Let's go and face the music shall we?" I say.

Sierra nods, her face back to normal. She leads the way into the chapel.

I follow Sierra into the chapel. It's not as bad inside as I was expecting. I'd been expecting a total cheese fest – heart shaped balloons, cupid statues, you name it, I was expecting it. Instead, it looks just like a small church.

A woman sitting at a small reception desk looks up at us as we enter. She must see the sheepish looks on our faces, or maybe she just sees regretful couples appearing first thing on a morning after pretty regularly, because she gives us a knowing smile as we approach her. "Trouble in paradise," she says.

"Something like that," Sierra agrees.

"You know, I shouldn't say this working in a place like this, but if I handled annulments instead of weddings, I could have retired rich years ago," she says.

She's hardly the warm and fuzzy approachable sort, but then again, neither am I and at least, she's not gushing about the sanctity of marriage.

"We're just trying to remember which chapel we got married in," I say. "Could you check your system and see if we were here last night please?"

She tries and fails to hide her smile. "Your names?"

"Chance Hunter and Sierra Lowe," I reply.

She raises one over plucked eyebrow. "Well, at least you know her second name. In this place, that makes you practically soul mates." She pulls out an ancient looking register from underneath her desk. She runs one red painted fingernail down a list of names and dates. "Nope. You didn't get married here," she says, shaking her head. "Sorry."

"Thanks for your help," I say, barely able to keep the sarcasm from my voice.

Sierra and I walk outside.

"Well, that was humiliating," she says. "And she was awful wasn't she?"

I nod my head. She was hardly the warm and friendly type I would have imagined organizing weddings.

"She was so cynical, like she doesn't believe in marriage or even love at all," Sierra adds.

I laugh softly. "Can you blame her for working here? I wonder how many people she sees like us every day. It's enough to make anyone a bit cynical."

"Well sure, but she should have learned to hide it," Sierra says. "And at least, we got a few brownie points for you actually knowing my name."

"See I'm a regular romantic!" I laugh.

Sierra laughs too and we begin to walk along the street towards the next chapel. It's only a few doors down and we're there in minutes.

Sierra reaches for the door and I touch her shoulder. "You wait here. I'll go in," I say.

She looks at me in surprise.

"I don't want you to feel humiliated like that again," I say.

She smiles and shakes her head. "I was just expecting... I don't know. A different attitude. I'm fine now. I know what to expect. Come on. We're in this together." She goes inside before I can respond.

I follow her in.

We're greeted by another small desk area with a woman sitting behind it. She smiles when she sees us, not the knowing smile of the other woman, just a friendly greeting and I relax a little.

"Good morning. Are you here as guests for the Carter and Miles wedding, or did you want to arrange your own wedding?"

"Wait, you have a wedding organized here with guests attending?" Sierra asks.

The woman frowns, looking confused. "You do know this is a chapel right?" she says.

"Yes. Sorry." Sierra laughs. "I just thought these places usually operated on a kind of spur of the moment sort of schedule."

"Oh, I see." The woman smiles. "Yes, we do get a lot of walk-ins, but some people actually choose Vegas as a venue. I mean it's the ideal venue in some ways. A ready- made place for your stag and bachelorette party, and a great place for a fun filled honeymoon without having to travel."

"I guess you're right," Sierra says. "Actually, we kind of already got married." She holds her hand up to show the woman the ring.

"Congratulations," she gushes.

I'm starting to think I preferred the cold cynicism of the other woman over this enthusiasm. It's ridiculous, but I somehow feel like I am letting this woman down by admitting that we screwed up badly.

"Yeah, thanks, but not really," Sierra says. "We were not exactly sober when it happened, and we're trying to work out where we got married, so we can get the marriage annulled."

"Ahh I see," the woman replies. "I'm sorry. You didn't get married here."

"How can you be sure? You don't even know our names," I interject.

"True. But I'm assuming the wedding was a spur of the moment thing and you didn't have your own rings?"

I nod my head.

"That's how I know," she says, nodding to Sierra's hand. "Our rings are all platinum and yours are gold."

"Oh," I say defeated.

The woman holds her hand out. "If I can see your ring, I might be able to help you," she offers.

Sierra slips her ring off and hands it to the woman.

I wonder for a moment why the hell we're both still wearing them. Until now, it never even occurred to me to take it off.

The woman looks at the ring and smiles. "It's from the Chapel of Endless Love," she says. "Turn left as you leave and just keep walking and you'll see it. It's not far from here, five minutes or so, if you're walking it."

Sierra takes the ring back and slips it back onto her finger.

Okay, so I can't exactly take mine off now, without risking offending her. I'll have to remember to take it off before I go back to the hotel though, offensive or not.

"How do you know?" Sierra asks.

"There are two interlinked hearts on the inside of the band. People generally think they're a romantic gesture. They're actually just the chapel's logo," she explains.

"Oh, I see," Sierra replies. "I did think it was a nice touch. But it's really just advertising. Wow. That's kind of sad isn't it? For the people who are in love I mean."

"I guess, but the symbol can mean whatever you want it to mean," the woman says.

"Thank you for your help." I smile at her. "We've taken up enough of your time."

"Yes, we have. And thank you," Sierra adds.

We turn to leave. Sierra stumbles slightly and I reach out my arm and catch her.

She laughs and shakes her head. "I guess the alcohol is still having an effect," she says.

"Or, you're just clumsy," I tease her.

"Yeah. It's more likely to be that," she says with a soft laugh.

I make sure Sierra is steady on her feet again, and then I release her arm, trying to ignore the tingles in my hand where my skin touched hers.

Sierra looks at her arm for a moment and then she drags her eyes away from the spot and takes a step forward.

I can't help but wonder if she felt the tingling too. I chastise myself, telling myself of course, she didn't. There was no tingling. It's just Vegas getting into my head.

"Wait," the woman says from behind us.

We stop and turn back to her. She's out of her seat and walking towards us. "I'm about to say something that's really out of line, and I hope you're not offended. I just wouldn't feel right if I didn't speak up."

Sierra and I exchange a glance and wait for the woman to go on.

She smiles. "I see hundreds of couples come through here every week and I've been doing this for a long time. We have many success stories, couples that are still deeply in love years after their wedding. And unfortunately, we have some sad stories too. Couples that grew apart, couples that fell out of love. And yes, some couples like you who realize they got caught up in the moment and made a mistake." She pauses looking uncomfortable suddenly.

Sierra and I exchange another glance.

The woman shrugs slightly with one shoulder. She has no idea where this is going either. "I'm sorry. I'm babbling. What I'm trying to say is I know love when I see it. And what you two have... well, it's not something I see in couples looking for an annulment. You have a connection."

I don't quite know what to say to this.

Sierra blushes next to me, going so red that the flush spreads down her neck and over her chest. "Well, the thing is, we're not strangers. We work together," Sierra explains. "So maybe that explains it."

"Maybe..." The woman smiles. "But let me tell you something else. I have a few male colleagues here. And not once have I ever looked at them like he looks at you."

"I..." I stop as suddenly as I started. What am I supposed to say to that? *I don't look at Sierra like anything. Do I?*

"I'm sorry. I shouldn't have said anything," the woman says when she sees how uncomfortable both Sierra and I are.

I finally find my voice, "It's okay. You haven't offended us. I just think your spidey senses are a little off on this one," I say.

"We'll see." She smiles. "Enjoy the rest of your time in Vegas."

She heads back to her desk.

Sierra and I hurry to get back outside. We step out into the sun and look at each other. We both burst into laughter at the same moment.

"Well, that was... intense," Sierra says.

"That's one word for it." I grin. "I think I preferred the cynic."

"Me too," Sierra agrees. "But at least now, we know where to go. No running in and out of every chapel along the street and getting insulted or paired off."

"I dread to think what we're going to find when we get to the Chapel of Endless Love," I say.

Sierra groans. "With a name like that, I bet we're in for one hell of an awkward conversation."

We turn left and start walking.

"They should have one called the Chapel of Regret," I joke. "Just to make the tourists feel at home."

"And one called the Chapel of Not Sure About This at All."

"Don't forget the chapel of *it seemed like a good idea at the time*."

"Or, the little chapel of *oh shit what have I done?*"

"The chapel of *we were bored of casinos*."

"*How drunk were we last night?*"

"How about the chapel of *fuck it, we're forty and single*."

"There should be a, *what happens in Vegas stays in Vegas* chapel. Where the marriage only counts while you're actually here."

"Yeah. There should be one of those on every corner!" I laugh.

"Maybe I should move out here and start a branding company aimed at chapels." Sierra giggles. "Instead of trying to sell the idea of eternal love, I'll sell the idea of it being one of those things you just have to do in Vegas. Like playing blackjack even if you've never played before."

"Or taking your assistant to a strip club, just because you can."

"Or eating at McDonalds because the nice places won't have you."

Or seeing someone in a new light... I think but don't say. What if that woman was right? What if Sierra and I do have a connection and we just didn't know it until now? I tell myself I'm getting caught up in the Vegas mood again. I mean what did she base her theory on exactly? The fact that Sierra tripped and I didn't let her face plant onto the ground? Surely, that doesn't mean anything except being a vaguely decent human being.

"Earth to Chance." Sierra laughs, pulling me out of my head.

"Sorry," I say. "I was a million miles away there." *Wondering if last night was really the mistake, or if in fact, what we're about to do is the mistake. Fucking hell, Chance, get a grip. Yesterday, you were pissed off because you had to drink shots and give up your work phone, and today you're debating the merits of marrying your assistant in a drunken moment of stupidity.*

Sierra points in front of her. "Look. The Chapel of Endless Love," she says.

"Right," I say. "Here we go. Prepare to become another statistic."

"Sounds fun." She grins.

We reach the building and I push the door open before I can let myself think any more about what we're doing. We enter the chapel, stepping into a little recess. An open door shows the chapel itself. White ribbons decorate the pews and a cascading arch of white roses stands at the altar. At least, we chose one of the nicer places. Maybe we weren't completely oblivious to our surroundings. Or maybe it was just random and we happened to glance up, see the sign, and think why not?

"Chance, Sierra, how's married life treating you," a woman says with a wide smile as she steps out of the main room of the chapel and into the little recess. "I wasn't expecting you until much later."

Sierra and I exchange another glance.

"You remember us?" Sierra asks.

"Of course!" The woman laughs. "Jane Kellerman? I officiated your wedding last night?"

"You seemed to be expecting us," I say.

"Well, yes," Jane replies, her smile slipping a little. "You said you'd be back today to pick up your certificate because you wanted to celebrate getting married and you were afraid you'd lose it."

"Wait," I say, a flash of hope going through me. "You mean we didn't sign any of the paperwork and we're not really married?"

Jane mistakes my hope for worry and she laughs and shakes her head. "Oh, don't worry. It's all official. You just left your copy here to collect. You must have had a really good celebration after you left here. You really don't remember any of this?"

"Honestly, we don't remember much of anything," Sierra admits. "We don't remember getting married. And we don't remember why we thought for even a second that would be a good idea."

Jane's face falls. "You mean you don't want to be married to each other?"

Sierra nods, blushing again. "Yeah. That's exactly what we mean."

Is her tone slightly sad or am I just imagining it? I'm probably imagining it and even if I'm not, she's probably just doing it for Jane's benefit. Somehow, it doesn't seem right to be laughing and full of joy while you're telling the woman who officiated your wedding that it was all just a big mistake.

"Come on through to my office. Let's talk," Jane says. She turns away from us and shouts, "Malcolm? Can you man the front desk for a bit, please? I need to take care of something."

A man about the same age as Jane appears. He greets us with a wide smile and then he sees Jane's expression and it fades slightly. "Is everything all right?" he asks.

"Not exactly," I say. "We're just trying to piece together last night."

"That good a night huh?" Malcolm asks.

"Come with me," Jane says, giving Malcolm a not so subtle look that tells him to stop asking questions.

He reads the look and shuts up, suddenly looking anywhere but at us.

Jane leads us through a door on her right and into her office. "Take a seat," she says, pointing to two chairs opposite hers behind her desk.

We all sit down.

Jane looks at us. "So, was I right out there?" she asks. "You regret the marriage?"

We both nod.

Jane looks so confused and I have to find out why. "I'm sorry to be blunt, but running a chapel in Vegas, surely you get this a lot."

"Less often than you might think," Jane says. "A lot of the chapels here will marry anyone, no matter how drunk they are. We do things a little differently here."

"But we were so drunk, we don't even remember last night," Sierra says.

"Maybe by the end of the night, but when you came here, you didn't seem to be intoxicated. I mean don't get me wrong, it was obvious you'd both had a drink, but you weren't falling around all over or slurring your words. And I didn't get the impression you two had just met. In fact, I know you hadn't because you told me as much. Two years is it?"

"We've known each for two years, yes," I say. "But we weren't in a relationship or anything."

"I know." Jane smiled. "You told me all about it. How you had worked together for two years and it took coming out to Vegas for business for you to see that you had real chemistry and that your relationship was so much more than just colleagues."

"That sounds kind of like drunken nonsense," Sierra says.

"It did to me at first too," Jane admits. "Until you told me the rest."

"The rest?" I prompt.

"Yes. How you threw yourself into work because you didn't think you'd ever find the one, and that she was right there in front of you all along, but by the time you realized you had feelings for her, you'd been working together so long, it would have made things awkward if you told her, in case she didn't feel the same. You really don't remember any of this?"

I shake my head. For once, it's me that's blushing rather than Sierra.

"You told me how your brother is getting married. You're here for his Bachelor party right? And how you thought it was stupid until you and Sierra talked and you said now you get it, but that you didn't want all of the fuss that came with Sebastian's wedding. You just wanted a quiet ceremony where you could celebrate your love for each other without having all of the frills."

Sierra looks at me out of the corner of her eye, looking surprised. She can't possibly be as surprised as I am by all of this.

"That doesn't sound like me at all," I say.

Jane shrugs. "Ultimately, it wasn't your words that convinced me you were for real. It was the way you were together. Looking at you two, all I could see was a deliriously happy couple, who had realized they were deeply in love and didn't want to waste another minute not being together. The way you looked at each other, the way you couldn't keep your hands off her."

Sierra smirks at me. "He couldn't keep his hands off me?" she says.

"Not even for a second. He touched your arm the whole time we were talking, and he kept stopping to kiss you." Jane smiles. "Honestly, I was starting to think he was going to walk down the aisle with you because he didn't seem to be able to bear the idea of not being by your side, even for those few minutes."

"Are you getting all of this Chance?" Sierra asks, giving me an innocent smile that is anything but innocent.

I can see the light dancing in her eyes. She's really enjoying the way Jane's words are making me squirm. I mean I know Jane has no reason to lie to us, but I can't imagine myself saying those words, or going on the way she is describing. It sounds like she's talking about someone else. The kind of someone else who would have me rolling my eyes and declaring them an idiot. "Loud and clear," I reply through gritted teeth.

Sierra just beams at me.

I turn my focus back to Jane. "So the thing is, the whole marriage thing was a mistake. And we need to get the marriage annulled. I know you seem to think we were all loved up and shit, but the truth is, we were just drunk."

"Maybe you should get him drunk again," Jane says to Sierra. "He was so much nicer than this last night."

Sierra giggles but then she turns serious. "Look we obviously had a good night and we were clearly in high spirits. But Chance is right. The wedding was a mistake and we really do want to get this whole thing sorted out."

"Okay," Jane says. She opens her top drawer and pulls out an envelope which she slides across her desk. "All of your certificates and things are in there. You'll need a notary and—"

"I have one arranged," Sierra cuts in. "But we need a witness who can testify to the fact that I was intoxicated. Who witnessed our wedding?"

Please not Matt. Please not Matt.

"You two came here alone," Jane says.

Thank God for that. At least one thing is going our way.

"I told you that you'd need two witnesses. Chance, you went out into the street and convinced a couple walking past to come in and act as your witnesses. Their contact details are on your paperwork."

"Thank you," Sierra says. She stands up.

I do the same and I nod my thanks to Jane.

"You know, it really is a shame to see you two ending your marriage. I honestly had you two pegged to be lifers," she says.

Why the hell do people keep saying that?

"You're actually the second person who has said that to us today," Sierra says.

Jane gives a soft laugh. "Sometimes, it takes outsiders to see what you can't see yourselves," she tells us.

I really wish people would stop confusing this matter. We made a mistake, we're fixing it. That's all there is to it. And the people who keep telling us we're in love or whatever, don't know us. They can't know more about us than we do. Can they?

I hate the uncertainty they're causing me to feel. I know how I feel about Sierra. She's a great assistant, amazing at her job. She's polite and kind. And apparently, she's funny, which granted, I didn't know until today. But that's it. She's not my soul mate. She's not my destiny or any of that shit. And we both know it.

We step back out into the street.

Sierra groans. "Why do I feel like we've somehow let Jane down? And why do I care?" she asks.

"I don't know but I know what you mean," I reply. "I feel exactly the same way." That's all it is that's making me a little confused about this. I feel bad for Jane, because she was so sure she was helping a loved up couple, rather than causing a problem for a drunken one.

"What are we like?" Sierra laughs. "We're the ones having to sort out this whole mess, we're the ones affected by it, and somehow, we both feel bad for someone else."

"It's Vegas!" I laugh. "It's making us crazy."

"You're right about that," Sierra says as she opens the envelope we were given and pulls out a few papers.

Our marriage certificate and a sheet of paper with the name, addresses and contact numbers of the couple who were apparently our witnesses.

"This is going to be a fun phone call," Sierra says as she hands me the certificate and envelope. She digs into her handbag and pulls out her phone. She types in the number and puts her phone on loudspeaker.

"Hello?" a man's voice says.

"Hi. Is this Gary Devon?" Sierra asks.

"Yeah. Who's this?"

"My name is Sierra Lowe, and ..."

"Sierra from last night? Wouldn't your name be Sierra Hunter now?"

Sierra and I look at each and she visibly winces.

"Yeah, about that," she says. "The whole wedding thing was a big mistake. We were drunk and stupid and I'm so sorry that you got pulled into this, but basically, we need to get this marriage annulled and I wondered if you would be willing to sign a form to testify that I was intoxicated at the time of getting married."

"I don't know," Gary replies, his tone a little nervous. "I mean I feel bad for you and everything, but I really don't want to get involved in your domestic life."

I realize what's happening. He thinks Sierra wants out of the marriage and is going behind my back to get it annulled. To be honest, until this morning, I would probably have thought the same thing in his position. I thought two people saying they didn't want to be married to each other should be enough, but apparently, it's much more complicated than that. "Gary, this is Chance," I say. "You're on loudspeaker. Don't worry, we're not having a domestic dispute. We're both in agreement that we want the marriage to be annulled but apparently that's not enough for the courts and if we don't have a witness to verify that Sierra was intoxicated at the time of the marriage, we'll have to go through the whole mess of getting a divorce rather than an annulment."

"Oh, I get you," Gary says. "Then sure, yeah, I'll sign your form."

"Thank you," Sierra and I say at the same time.

"I have a notary who can witness us signing the papers today. Can you text us the address of the best place to meet you?" Sierra goes on.

"Yeah, no worries. It's a shame though. You guys seemed so in love," Gary says then ends the call.

Sierra and I look at each other again.

She rolls her eyes. "You know the stupidest part of all of this?" Sierra says. "If we'd been married for two years and where getting a divorce, no one would question it or tell us how good we are together."

"True," I say. My phone starts to ring. I pull it out of my pocket and check the screen. "It's Sebastian," I say.

"Take it," Sierra says. "They're going to get suspicious if they go up to your room looking for you and you're not there. Go back to the hotel and be there for your brother. I can take care of this."

"Are you sure? I mean I feel kind of bad leaving you to fix this mess on your own," I say.

"I'm your assistant. Fixing your messes is kind of my job." She laughs. "Now go, before I change my mind."

"Thanks, you're the best." I start to walk away from her and I take the call. I glance back over my shoulder and see Sierra walking away from me. I watch her as she walks, the way her hips move beneath her clothes. The way she holds her back straight and her head up high, confident in herself but not arrogant.

"Chance? Where the hell are you?" Sebastian asks instead of saying hello.

"Wow, have you missed me that much?" I laugh. "I woke up with the hangover from hell, so I went for a walk to get some air. What are you even doing up?"

"It's almost twelve Chance," Sebastian points out.

I go to argue with him – it can't be that late – but when I check my watch, I see that he's right.

"Just come back to the hotel and meet us for lunch okay?" Sebastian says.

"On my way," I tell him. I end the call and look around for a cab. I can't take the forty-five minutes to arrive that it would take to walk back from here without raising some suspicions. I manage to find a cab and I give the cab driver the address of a hotel two doors up the street from ours. It will also look damned suspicious if any of them see me getting out of a cab too.

Chapter Nine

SIERRA

I slip my ring off and push it down deep into the front pocket of my jeans as I make my way to our hotel. I stroll through the doors of the hotel, making sure I appear casual in case I'm spotted. I glance around the lobby. No one is waiting for me.

Of course, they aren't.

They don't suspect anything. I'm just being paranoid. They just think I got too drunk and overslept. They'll tease me about it, I'll get mad and remind them it was their stupid idea for me to drink so much, and that will be the end of it

I cross the lobby heading for the restaurant. I go inside. It's nice and cool and it's still pretty quiet. I easily spot Sebastian and the others crowded around a table in the far corner of the room. It's a buffet lunch. They've filled their plates and are chowing down.

Matt spots me and gives me a wave.

I wave back and then point to the buffet, letting them know I'm going to get some food and then I'll be joining them. I go over to the buffet. I didn't think I was hungry until I saw all of the food, but now that I can see it and smell it, I am suddenly ravenous. It's how I always am after I've had a good drink the night before. I don't understand these people that can't eat after a night out. I wonder briefly if Sierra will have time to stop and grab a bite to eat and I wonder if I should text her and check in on her. I tell myself she's a grown woman. She can decide for herself if she wants to stop and eat or not.

I help myself to a cheeseburger and a plate full of fries. It's not exactly high cuisine, but it's what my body is craving. I smile to myself when I think of Sierra trying to convince us all to go for burgers last night because the restaurants are just a rip off.

I push all of my hazy thoughts of last night away as I turn and walk towards the others. I just need to act normal and no one will suspect a thing. "How's everyone's heads then?" I ask as I sit down and poke a fry into my mouth.

I get back a series of groans and moans which tells me I might be the only one with a new wife, but I'm not the only one suffering from a hangover.

"It's good to see you're in one piece anyway," Matt says.

I frown as I munch on my burger. "Why wouldn't I be?" I ask.

"Well, no reason, but being that we lost you at like eleven o'clock, it's just good to know you're okay," Matt replies.

"You lost me at eleven?" I ask. "I don't remember much from last night to be honest."

"Yeah. We went for burgers at McDonalds because stupid here couldn't keep his mouth shut," Matt says, nodding towards Sebastian. "And then we went to that strip joint. It was a bat shit, so we left after a cocktail or two. Somewhere between leaving the strip club and getting to the next one, you and Sierra were gone."

"Shit. I forgot about Sierra," Sebastian says. "Someone should really check on her."

"I'll go check on her." Rick grins.

I glare at him until he looks away.

"She's fine. I saw her this morning," I say. "I gave her the morning off and she'll be working this afternoon. And I don't want any comments about that, Seb."

Sebastian holds his hands up and shakes his head. "After the partying you did last night, my work here is done. You sure as hell weren't thinking about work." He grins.

"So, you have no idea where you ended up after you left us?" Matt says.

"Oh, yeah. I went back to the hotel and had a few drinks in the bar before going to bed," I say. "I was just surprised it was so early when we left the strip club. I thought it was later."

"We'd been drinking since lunch time though," Mark reminds me.

"So what did you guys get up to then?" I ask.

"Oh, you missed the best part," Matt says. "We went into this bar and they had one of those mechanical bull things going. Sebastian insisted on us all taking a turn. Mark ended up needing stitches and Bradley now holds the record for staying on the bull the longest."

"You had to get stitches?" I ask Mark.

He nods and grins, holding up his hand and showing me a stitched cut on his palm. "It was no big deal. They had one of those mobile first aid stations just down the street. They patched me up and I got right back on it. The drink that is. Not the bull. The bull can fuck off." He laughs.

"We went on to another casino after that," Rick puts in. "Lost a couple of grand. And then a couple more bars and strip clubs."

I sit listening to their stories as we eat, laughing along and finding myself shocked by some of the stories they're telling. Not as shocked as they'd be if they heard my story though. My mind wanders back to Sierra and I wonder if she's managed to get the papers filed yet. God, I hope the court will just grant this damned thing and we don't have to mess with getting a proper divorce.

As I think of Sierra, I see her in my mind's eye, her hair loose around her face and her skin looking oh, so soft. I remember how I touched her arm to steady her in one of the chapels we visited and how I got tingles along my skin when I touched her.

I think of her laugh. It's a lovely sound. Musical and infectious and full of innocent wonder and joy. Has it always sounded like that? How did I not notice it before today? I suppose in the same way that I didn't notice how her eyes sparkle when she tells a joke. I've never really looked before. Yet today, I started to look, to really see Sierra as more than just my assistant.

I mean of course, we can't just stay married. I don't see her as my wife. But I do see her as... something. Something more than just background noise in the office. Something that makes me want to smile when I think of her. Something that makes me let my guard down and just live in the moment and laugh.

I realize with a start that Sebastian was right about last night. I didn't think about work once. And it wasn't just last night. I haven't thought about it once this morning either. I tell myself it's because right now I have bigger problems, but even as I try to convince myself that's all it is, I know it's more than that. It's Sierra. When I'm with her, nothing seems so serious. It's like she infects me with joy. Like all I can think about is her when I'm with her.

Shit, stop it Chance. This is really fucking dangerous ground.

Knowing this doesn't stop me from seeing Sierra in my mind though, her eyes twinkling, laughter on her lips. I wonder what her lips would taste like. Dammit, I might already know.

It's killing me not being able to remember what happened between us last night. Did we have sex or not? If we did, what did her body feel like in my arms? What does she taste like? How soft would her skin feel against my hands, against my tongue? What did her pussy feel like wrapped around my cock? Did I make her feel good?

So many questions and where the answers should be, there is only a blur. I want so badly to remember, but wanting something doesn't always make it happen. I have to let this go before the not knowing drives me completely crazy.

The guys are still talking, comparing notes about who had the wildest time last night, who drank the most, who lost the most money in the casino. Not Sierra. She still had the chips in her bag this morning to prove it. And just like that—she's in my head again. My fingers move down to my pocket of their own accord, rubbing over the denim and feeling the gold band inside.

I can't let myself get all crazy like this. Whatever happened last night shouldn't have happened at all. That's all there is to it. And the whole wedding thing was obviously a mistake. The rational and crazy sides of my brain could both agree on that one. Marrying someone after spending one fun night together is ridiculous. And we do need to annul the marriage.

Sebastian is recounting a story about a stripper who wanted to take him out the back and give him a private lap dance and I laugh along and make all of the right noises, but inside, I'm rolling my eyes at the story. And that's when it hits me. I'm missing Sierra's company.

With her, I don't feel like I'm acting, taking on the role of someone I should be, the role of who those around me want me to be. I'm just me. And she seems okay with that.

I imagine myself pushing my fingers into Sierra's hair, feeling how soft and silky it is against my fingers. I move closer, my lips brushing hers, and then it's like we've both been unleashed. Our hands are all over each other, ripping each other's clothes off, and I'm kissing her, tasting her, inhaling her. I throw her on the bed—

"Chance?" Sebastian says.

His voice pulls me out of my head. I remember where I am and I start a little when I realize my cock is starting to get hard. "What?" I ask Sebastian, focusing on him and not on my daydreaming.

His face does the trick and my hard on goes away.

"You're acting awfully strange," Matt says, narrowing his eyes and peering at me like all of my secrets are laid bare on my face if he could just work out how to read them.

"I don't know what you're talking about," I say. "I'm just hungover." I can feel my face turning red even as I say it.

All of them are staring at me now.

I shift uncomfortably in my seat. God, this is worse than hearing the stories from last night. Way, way worse.

"He's probably mentally planning his next work phone call once lunch is done." Matt laughs.

Sebastian shakes his head. "No. He's not. I know that look. He's not thinking about work at all. He's thinking about a woman."

The others all readily agree.

"You know what? You're right." Matt grins. "Look at how red his face is. Wow bro, is there more to you than just work? I was starting to think you would die a virgin."

"Haha, very funny," I say.

"He's not a virgin. Remember Josie Lees?" Sebastian says.

"Oh, yeah. She was Chance's first love," Matt tells the others.

They begin to tell stories about my awkward teen years.

I laugh along, pleased the conversation has moved on from where my mind was moments ago. I tell myself to stay focused and not go off into my head again. That was way too close for comfort.

"I told you he was thinking about a woman," Sebastian says after a few minutes of them ribbing me.

How the hell did he get to that conclusion? I've laughed along, practically hung on every word.

Even Matt looks confused now.

"He's always got mad when we bring Josie up," Sebastian notes. "And now, he's laughing along with us. Because he wants to deflect attention away from the real issue here. *Who* he is thinking about."

Dammit. Am I so easy to read?

"We've all been telling our stories about what happened last night, but I think Chance has the best one and he's holding back on us, pretending like he doesn't remember. Come on Chance. Spill. Who is she?"

I should just make something up. Tell them how I met a woman in the hotel bar and went up to her room. I don't want to do that though. I don't want to feed into their stupidity. And if it gets back to Sierra that I've been telling these kinds of stories, what will she think? She'll think I remember what happened between us and I held back because I was ashamed of her or something. And she'll think I've been telling the guys stories about what we did.

"Aww, he's gone all shy." Mark laughs. "She must be the one or something."

"Bullshit," Bradley puts in. "You saw how pissed he was. I bet he doesn't even remember her name. Is that what it is?"

I search my mind frantically, trying to come up with something to say. I settle on a half-truth. "I honestly don't remember much of what happened after the strip club. I don't even remember losing you guys," I say in what I hope is a casual, normal tone.

Sebastian is still staring at me like he's trying to figure something out.

I glare at him, warning him with my eyes not to push this.

As usual, Sebastian ignores me. Suddenly, his face changes and his mouth drops open. "Oh, fuck. It was Sierra wasn't it? You brought her back here and showed her what a good boss you can be!"

All of their eyes are on me again.

I can feel my face heating up again. "That's enough," I say quietly. "That's my assistant you're talking about. Have a bit of fucking respect."

"Ooh, you've touched a nerve." Mark chuckles.

"Yeah, he's defending her honor," Matt puts in.

Rick is nodding his head now. "It explains why you got so heated about me hitting on her in the lobby. Shit man, I'm sorry. I didn't know you two were a thing. I wouldn't have said anything if I'd known."

"We're not a thing," I say, far too quickly, almost before Rick has even finished what he's saying. I'm not lying. *We're not a thing.* And when Rick was hitting on Sierra, nothing had even happened between us. I just didn't want him making her uncomfortable.

"Oh, you *so* are a thing," Matt says. He pauses, studying my face, as I try my best to keep my expression neutral, bored even, like I am so over this conversation for reasons other than it touching a raw nerve.

"Or maybe, they're not. Maybe it was just a drunken mistake," Matt adds.

Oh God, if only they knew.

"So?" Sebastian demands, turning to me. "Which is it?"

"It's neither. And as always, it's none of your fucking business," I snap.

I know I'm making things worse. The more I snap at them and get all defensive, the more they know they're touching a nerve. I try to imagine how I would have acted if it wasn't true. I would have just stared at them blankly, more shocked than annoyed. I've blown it completely.

"Sierra's cute," Bradley puts in.

Not helping. If I agree, it's only going to set them off again. But I can't say she isn't, because, well, she is. Bradley's eyes are twinkling and I realize he knew he was dropping a bomb. "Yeah, she is," I say. "So is the waitress and I'm not going to go hit on her."

"Because Sierra wouldn't like that," Matt says.

I sigh as I shake my head and decide to have one last attempt at ending this, "Sierra is my assistant. Just think about that for a moment. Even if I had wanted to hit on her, I wouldn't have. At best, she might have responded and that would have made it awkward as hell when we go back to work. At worst, she sues me for sexual harassment. Why would I risk either?"

"Because love works in mysterious ways," Sebastian says. "And you *love her*," he says in a sing-song voice and starts blowing air kisses.

I've heard enough. I get up from the table quickly. "Excuse me, gentlemen. I think I've heard enough," I say coldly.

This gets a chorus of whoops that I ignore. I start to walk away.

"Oh come on. We're only messing with you," Sebastian calls after me.

I keep my head held high, but I keep walking. Running footsteps catch up with me in the hallway and as they reach me, they slow down to match mine. I glance to the side and see Matt.

"You know they're only going to wind you up more now, don't you?" Matt says.

"I don't care." I shrug.

"Yeah, you do, or you wouldn't have stormed off," Matt counters.

"I didn't storm off," I retort. "I walked away because I don't think it's right that you're all discussing an employee like she's a piece of meat."

Matt looks away for a second and I think he's actually ashamed of himself, but then he looks back at me.

Now, I see the smile forming across his lips.

"You know, none of us really believed you were with Sierra. It was just a way to get a reaction. But now I see it. We were right weren't we?"

"You've had your bit of fun Matt. Can we just fucking drop it now?" I hiss.

"Just tell me what happened. I won't tell the others. Are you like, into her, or was it just a one night thing?"

"Seeing as this is only happening in your own imagination, that's a question only you can answer," I reply.

Matt's grin widens. "Oh come on, spill. Or I can always ask Sierra."

"You wouldn't dare!" I snap.

"Oh, really? Try me," Matt challenges.

I stop walking and turn to glare at Matt.

He just smirks at me. "I know your scary face works on employees bro, but that's because you can fire them. Your nasty little look isn't going to scare me."

I keep looking at him for a moment longer and then I turn and walk away.

He calls after me, but this time, he at least has the good sense not to follow me.

I don't look back and before I reach the end of the hallway, I hear him walking back towards the restaurant.

I stalk towards the elevator. I don't know how this has gotten so out of hand. I knew I should have just stayed at home and let the others come out here to Vegas without me. Then none of this would have happened, and the only jokes I'd be getting fired at me would be ones about being boring, a workaholic and old before my time. All the standard ones I'm used to and don't worry me at all.

My mind is whirling with awful possibilities. What if Matt really does ask Sierra about last night? Will she assume I told him and talk? No, surely not. If she thinks I told him, she'll be furious with me, but it doesn't mean she's about to start talking to Matt about her sex life.

I know deep down, no one will ask her about it. It's one thing winding me up and making me uncomfortable, but they wouldn't do that to Sierra. Would they? I know Matt and even Sebastian wouldn't. They enjoy my discomfort, but they know where the line is with employees, and asking them about their sex life, real or imagined, is well and truly over the line.

I step into the elevator car and push my hand into my pocket. I rub my fingers over the ring there, and somehow, I feel calmer. I smile to myself when I think of Sierra laughing in the cab earlier.

I pull my hand away from the ring and tell myself to nip this in the bud right now. It's going to be hard, but I have to go back to seeing Sierra as nothing but my assistant. It doesn't matter that when I think of her now, I see her beautiful eyes sparkling, or that I imagine myself running my hands over her body.

I have to go back to cold and professional, because if either of my brothers see even the tiniest flicker of warmth between us, they're never going to let this go.

Chapter Ten

SIERRA

It's been a long morning and I'm glad to get back to my room and kick my shoes off. I sit down on the bed and massage my feet for a moment. I'm debating taking a shower and changing into something a little cooler, but I know Chance will be coming along soon to go over the files and I don't want him to think our little moment has made me lax about work. Will he still think of me as professional if he comes in and I'm wearing casual clothes? I doubt it.

I decide to stay in my skirt and blouse. It's not like I'm not used to it. It drives me mad at the office when it's hot and half of the staff think it's okay to let their standards slip. I'm not going to start doing the same thing. Even if we are in Vegas.

I open my laptop and begin the work I've been given. It's not so bad. It's easy work. Time consuming, but not something I really have to think about. My mind flits away from the task at hand and goes to Chance. He really is hot. I don't know how I never saw it before. I mean I knew he was handsome, but I never really thought of him as someone desirable. Until now. Because apparently, waking up in someone's bed and seeing them naked... definitely changes how you see them.

And spending the morning laughing at our predicament helped too. It was nice to feel like for once, I had a problem and I wasn't in it alone.

A couple of hours go by and there's a knock at my door. I get up, telling myself I can't feel the butterflies in my stomach and that my heart isn't racing wildly as I approach the door. I run my hands over my skirt, and then I pat my hair to make sure it's in place.

Not for Chance. I don't care what he thinks. Much.

I pull the door open and I am assaulted by the sight of him. He towers over me, and his shoulders are wide. He looks like the sort of man who makes everything okay. I imagine stepping into his arms and leaning my head back, so he can kiss me. I imagine how I would feel wrapped up in his body, his cock slamming into me. I catch myself and clear my throat.

Chance is looking back at me and I'm sure that for a second, I see desire in his eyes. He blinks and it's gone; he's all business again. But it was there. I swear it was there. I'm not exactly known for being someone who has flights of fancy. If I saw it, it happened. It doesn't matter though. Nothing can happen between Chance and me. We had our chance and neither of us remember it and that's just a regret I'll have to live with, because there won't be another episode.

"Good afternoon," I smile, standing back from the door.

Chance returns my smile and steps into the room. "Did you get the signatures?" he asks.

I nod my head. "Yes. The papers are all complete and they've been filed. It's just a waiting game now. Everything was more than in order, and the notary said he'd be surprised if they didn't grant the annulment. It would just be a waste of every-one's time and resources if they made a big deal out of it."

"Perfect, thank you," Chance says curtly.

So we're back to this. Mr. cool, calm and professional. I can live with that. It'll make ignoring the throbbing feeling between my legs much easier. I wonder briefly if I should go back to calling him Mr. Hunter, but that would surely be weird now. I mean he's tried to convince me to call him Chance for long enough, even before any of this happened.

"Where are we with work?" Chance asks, moving to sit down on the edge of the bed.

"Getting there," I say. "I've spent the last few hours working on sourcing the things you wanted."

"You'll have them all by the end of the day?" he asks curtly, his eyebrow raised.

Okay, I thought I was alright with this – with going back to how things were, but I'm not. I'm not okay with it at all. Chance finally warmed up and showed me the man beneath the mask and I liked what I saw. I actually let myself believe we would have fun for the rest of the weekend, but that's clearly out of the window. And to be honest, I don't appre-ciate his tone or the raised eyebrow. It's not like I've been laying around the pool all fucking morning.

"Probably not," I say. "I haven't had the time to really dive into the more complicated ones. You know, because I spent the morning running around the strip, trying to get our marriage annulled."

Chance's face softens slightly. "Yeah, I get it. Sorry. It's just, this is important," he says.

"I know. Just like you know I've never missed a deadline. And I don't intend to start now. Everything you've asked for will be on your desk first thing Monday morning."

"Good. There's one more thing," he says.

This is it. He's going to go back to being human Chance and say something nice.

He raises an eyebrow and looks pointedly at my laptop.

I realize I have it all wrong. He means one more thing he wants me to do for work. I remind myself I am being paid quite handsomely to be here. I'm not here for a vacation. That was never on the cards. I need to snap out of this assumption that Chance and I are going to be anything other than what we've always been.

I move to the laptop and pick it up. I sit down on the bed, perching it on my knee. Chance begins to talk, telling me what he needs me to do. There's really nothing in the instructions that I can't remember and I don't bother noting any of them down. I just listen, or rather, I let the sound of his voice, low and masculine, wash over me, while I desperately try to ignore the way my pussy is getting wetter and wetter as I look at Chance.

Finally, he stops talking and looks at me questioningly.

"What?" I say, aware of his gaze on my face. I can feel myself flushing under his gaze and I force myself to look away from his eyes, even though they try to hold me in place.

"I'm just wondering why you're not taking any of this down," he says. His voice has changed, his sentences short and clipped like he's trying and failing to hide his anger at me.

Well, my boss or not, he doesn't get to play that card. We were both there last night. He fucked up every bit as much as I did. I stand up and take my laptop to the small table in the corner of the room and then I turn back to Chance. "And I'm just wondering if you even remember a time when your life wasn't consumed by work. I mean you're in Vegas for God's sake and all you can think about is work."

"Excuse me?" Chance asks his gaze looking angry.

Good. It's nice to know he can still feel something.

"Look, despite last night, our relationship is strictly business and nothing has changed between us," he says.

"Are you sure about that?" I challenge him.

He stares at me again, his face unreadable.

I decide to elaborate before he thinks I'm trying to have sex with him. "Because before this, you've always trusted me to do what you ask of me. Not once have I ever taken more than a note or two when you give me instructions. And not once, have I ever let you down. You've never questioned my methods before, yet now, you seem to think I need to write down everything you say."

I see the realization dawn on his face and I'm slightly vindicated when he has the decency to look a little ashamed of himself.

"You're right. I'm sorry," he says. "So where was I?"

"You were about to tell me about a time when you just let go, had fun and did something you wanted to do outside of work," I say. I know it's a risk saying it, but I feel like we've moved past this stiff interaction. I've always thought of Chance as a happy workaholic. Someone who works too hard because they choose to. But this morning, I saw a glimpse of a man who wants more. Who wants to not be chained to his desk all day. Who actually has personality.

He jumps up off the bed, and for a second, I think I've misjudged the situation horribly. I've massively overstepped the mark and Chance is angry with me. Like really angry I feel a shiver run through my body as he moves so gracefully, lithe yet strong. The shiver I feel isn't fear though. It's desire. Chance's size and his smoldering anger doesn't scare me. It turns me on.

"You realize your questions are totally out of line, right?" he says.

He doesn't sound as angry as I imagined and I decide to push it a little but further. "See that's the thing. They're not. I'm not asking you about anything deeply personal. I'm asking you to tell me about a time you had fun. That's it. It's not inappropriate. Colleagues talk to each other."

He sighs and sits back down, the anger gone completely now. "Running a business isn't about having fun Sierra. I can't just give in to my every desire or let emotions rule me. I know to some people that sounds miserable, but to me, it's just the way it is. Yes, I've made sacrifices in my personal life, but the business wouldn't be where it is today if I hadn't."

"But at what point do you say yes, I've made it, now I can actually have a life?" I ask.

His eyes are fixed on mine again, and I know this time it's definitely desire I can see in them. I start to walk slowly towards him. I try to stop myself, but I can't. It's like my feet are on autopilot just moving me towards him.

"I don't know," Chance admits. "Every time I think about it my mind just refuses to answer. I can't just start making stupid decisions now."

"I agree," I say. "But I don't think having a little fun every now and then is stupid." I'm still moving towards him. I stop when I'm a foot away and gaze into his eyes. "I think giving in to your desires now and again, and letting yourself have some fun is the reward for working so hard."

My voice is low and husky, dripping with sex. I barely recognize it as my own voice, and I like how it sounds. It sounds powerful, like the voice of a woman who knows what she wants and knows how to get it. I can feel my breath coming quickly, my chest heaving as I look down at Chance. His eyes lock on mine and I see a whirl of emotions. Desire. Panic. Indecision. His breathing is coming as fast as mine and his eyes don't leave mine for even a second.

The indecision fades from his eyes, the panic leaving them and his lips curl up into a smile. All that's left on his face now is desire. He's bold and unashamed as he reaches out and wraps one arm around my waist. He pulls me closer to him and I find myself pressed against his chest. Even sitting, he's almost as high as I am and I only have to tilt my head slightly to be able to gaze into his eyes.

He reaches up with his other hand and cups it around the back of my neck, pulling my face down to meet his. His lips press against mine and I feel desire explode through my body as our lips move as one. I reach out and wrap my arms around him, moving my hands up and down his back, desperate to feel his bare skin against mine but stopped by his shirt.

His tongue moves across my lips, pushing into my mouth as he deepens the kiss. I can feel the pent up frustration, the passion he tries to keep hidden. My body explodes with longing, my clit throbbing, my pussy wetter than it's ever been. My body responds to Chance like we've always been this way; like this is the most natural thing in the world. Maybe it is and we've just never allowed ourselves to see it before now.

My nipples are rock hard and I can feel them pressing against Chance's chest, sending little shock waves through my body. My heart is racing as I explore Chance's tongue with my own.

His hand moves down from my waist, resting on my ass then pushing my body tighter against his.

I moan into his mouth as he lights my whole body on fire. I have never wanted anyone as fiercely and as completely as I want Chance now.

As abruptly as he started to kiss me, he stops. He puts his hands on my hips and holds me out at arm's length. We stare at each other, our chests heaving. Chance's eyes seemed to have darkened as lust fills him, and I feel my pussy clench at the sight of them. I need to feel his cock inside of me, rocking my world.

"Sierra," he says.

I know if I let him finish that sentence, this will be over. The rational side of him will take over, pushing his more primal side back to dormant. I can't let that happen. I have to have him.

I reach down and pull my blouse out of my skirt. I lift it over my head and throw it to one side in one easy movement. I stand before him in my bra, watching his reaction. I sweep my eyes over his body and even through his trousers I can see his cock is hard, ready for me.

"It seems a shame that we finally let our hair down and neither of us remember it," as I speak, I reach up and unclip my hair, letting it fall around my shoulders. I shake my head from side to side, shaking my hair out.

Chance lets out a low growling sound and gets to his feet. I don't back up and he's standing there, his body almost touching mine.

He growls again and reaches up and strokes my hair. "It does seem like a shame," he says in a husky voice that makes my pussy throb. "I think we should fix that." He takes a half step back and in a blur of movement, his shirt is coming off. He bends down and grabs at his shoes and socks.

I don't need telling twice. I reach around and unbutton my skirt, letting it fall to the ground, kicking it away.

Within seconds, we're facing each other again, both of us only in our underwear.

I know if this happens, there's no going back. I don't want to go back. I want to feel Chance's hands all over my body. His tongue on me, his cock in me. I want him to claim my pussy and fill me up.

I feel as though Chance is reading my mind the way he is completely focused on me, but in truth, I think my need for him is written all over my face. He reaches out and grabs me, lifting me off the ground. He turns and throws me onto the bed. I scoot backwards a little, making room for him. He gets onto the bed and lowers his body over mine. I am consumed by him, his scent filling my nostrils, his touch sending electricity through my body.

I reach up for him, but he grabs my wrists. He pulls my arms above my head and holds them in place with one hand. He rubs his other hand gently over my face and then his eyes darken again and any sense of gentle is gone. He leans closer and begins to run his tongue over my neck.

I lean my head back, exposing the sensitive skin there to his touch. Goosebumps scurry over my body as he nips my skin between his teeth, making me feel more alive than I have ever felt before.

Chapter Eleven

CHANCE

I don't really know how this happened, I only know I don't want it to stop. My head has been filled with Sierra since I came back to the hotel, and now all of my senses are full of her. I can taste her skin as I run my tongue over her neck. I can smell the strawberry scent of her hair. I can feel her effect in every cell in my body.

I want to consume her, to slam my cock into her and claim her pussy right now. But I know this time, she won't forget and I want her to remember something worthwhile. I want to make her come over and over again, to make her body sing. I want her screaming my name as her body goes wild beneath my touch. I want her to remember me as a lover who made her feel good.

I run my tongue lower, moving it down along her chest. She arches her back into my touch and I put my free hand beneath her, unhooking her bra. I release her wrists long enough to pull it off her and throw it to one side, and then I pin her arms in place again. I kiss her mouth, a frantic, desperate kiss that she returns with as much desire as I feel for her.

I move my tongue down her neck and chest again. I release her hands as I move lower, sucking one of her nipples into my mouth.

She moans loudly and pushes her hands into my hair, holding me in place on her breast.

I move my tongue back and forth against her rock hard nipple, feeling it press down at my touch and then spring back up again, filling my mouth with the essence of her.

Sierra writhes beneath me, moaning, eager for more.

My cock is so hard it's almost uncomfortable and I can feel the heat coming off her pussy, washing over my cock in waves that makes me wild. I can't wait any longer. I have to taste her pussy, taste her lust. I move my tongue down over her stomach, my hands staying on her breasts. I knead her breasts, feeling her hard nipples against my palms.

I watch as her skin puckers where my tongue runs over it. I reach her pussy and grab her panties in my teeth. I pull my head back hard, tearing them away from her body and exposing her glistening mound.

I look at her pussy for a moment, appreciating the fact that I have done this to her. I have made her dripping wet and undone her completely. But she has undone me as much as I've undone her. I feel unrestricted, like nothing matters but this woman and her pleasure.

I lean my head down, my tongue finding her dripping wet clit. I taste Sierra's juices, musky and salty sweet. I moan against her clit and she bucks her hips against my tongue as I work her clit. I move my hands from her breasts, running them down her body and settling them on her hips. I hold her hips in place as I work her. She moans loudly, sending waves of desire through me. She lifts her leg, wrapping it around my shoulders, pushing my face deeper into her warm folds.

I go to town on her clit, licking back and forth, side to side, nibbling on it and sending her wild. I can feel it pulsing against my tongue, can smell the lust running from her pussy as I send her over the edge.

She screams my name, her body tensing up. Her leg presses so tightly against my neck that for a moment, my face is mashed against her and I can't breathe.

I don't care. I don't need oxygen, I need Sierra. This much is blatantly clear to me now.

She moves her hips, rubbing her pulsing clit across my face and her leg relaxes. I pull back a little, gasping in a breath and then I continue my assault on Sierra's clit. Her hands reach down and grab two fistfuls of my hair, pulling on it as she screams my name again. The stinging sensation in my scalp seems to go straight to my cock and I know I can't hold back much longer.

I move my tongue through Sierra's lips, pushing it inside of her pussy. Her pussy clenches around it, and she moans loudly.

"Oh my God, Chance," she breathes as her pussy clenches again.

I press against her clit with my fingers as I move my tongue in and out of her, lapping it around the edges of her pussy.

She comes again, washing my face in her juices and I eagerly lap them up, drinking her in.

I come up onto my knees and look down at her face contorted in agonizing ecstasy as her orgasm rips through her. Her skin is flushed, a sheen of sweat standing out on her body. She has never looked so good as she does now. She is mine and I intend to take her right now.

I push my boxer shorts down and wriggle out of them as Sierra's eyes open and her face relaxes. She gives me a sated smile, her eyes looking glassy. I lean forward and mash my mouth against hers. She responds to my kiss, her hands all over my body as her tongue wraps itself around mine. I know she is tasting her own pleasure, and the taste seems to spur her on.

She pushes a hand between us, grabbing my cock and rubbing it expertly.

If she keeps doing that, I'm going to come too quickly and I grab her wrist and pull her hand away from me.

Her eyes fly open, looking panicked at first but then she smiles when she sees the way I'm looking at her.

I lift myself up from her and grab my cock, lining it up with Sierra's pussy. I can feel how wet she is; how much she wants this. I tease her, rubbing my cock around the edge of her pussy.

"Chance, please," she gasps, her eyes on mine.

"Please what?" I grin, enjoying the moment, enjoying how much she wants me.

"Fuck me," she says.

Her words flash through my mind like a red hot poker and I can't stop myself now. I slam into her pussy as she throws her head back and sucks in a tortured sounding breath. I can feel her pussy opening for me as I lower my body gently back onto hers. I touch her cheek and then I kiss her again. A deep, passionate kiss that sends tingles down my spine.

She wraps her legs around my waist, her arms lock around my shoulders.

I have never felt closer to anyone than I do at this moment. She is me and I am her. I move inside of her, my cock going wild as her tight little pussy clamps around me, pulling me in deeper, making me fill her up. I up my pace, moving quickly through her hot, wet tunnel, feeling every clench of her walls.

I kiss her neck and then I pull my head up to look at her as I feel her pussy lock around my cock.

She is coming hard, her eyes rolling back in her head. She goes floppy for a second, but my next thrust pulls her back and her eyes roll back into place. She throws her head back, barely able to breathe as pleasure fills her.

I can feel my own climax building rapidly and I know I won't be able to hold back for much longer. I slam into Sierra again, feeling her wrapped around me. My cock twitches as fire roams freely around my body. I suck in a breath then slam into her again and my cock spurts, freeing my seed, filling Sierra with heat.

I gasp again and moan her name as I come hard. Her pussy is still clenching around me, drawing my orgasm out, making it last until I feel it in every part of my body. Slowly, it begins to fade and I kiss the tip of Sierra's nose and roll off her.

I lay on my back panting, listening to Sierra's ragged breaths beside me. Aftershocks of pleasure fire through my body and I close my eyes, enjoying the feeling of warmth that spreads through me, wanting it to last forever.

It seems Sierra was right. Sometimes, just letting go and doing what you want to do really is the best thing in the world.

Sierra rolls onto her side and shuffles closer to me and I lift my arm up. She rests her head on my chest and I hold her tightly against me. I can feel her heart racing against my side.

She puts her palm on my stomach and gently moves it in a lazy circle. "Well, I for sure won't forget that," she says in a breathy voice.

"Me neither," I assure her.

I have a feeling I'll be thinking about Sierra for a whole hell of a long time to come.

I stand at the window and look outside onto the grounds of Moorfield Mansion. The grounds are exquisite; manicured lawns, perfectly arranged flower beds, tall trees that sway slightly in the breeze. The pink blossoms of cherry trees floating down lazily on the breeze and leaving a carpet of pink. There's a small creek running through the bottom of the grounds with an ornate brick bridge over it.

Sebastian and Kimberley have really chosen the perfect picturesque venue for their wedding.

The ceremony will take place on the grounds and I can see staff members rushing around arranging white chairs with large pink satin bows tied around them in rows on either side of the red carpeted aisle. A white arch decorated with greenery and white and pink roses stands at the end of the aisle. Sebastian and Kimberley will stand beneath it to say their vows.

The reception will take place in the ballroom of the mansion, and as most of the guests are staying over in the rooms in the mansion, the reception will go late.

As I stand looking out over the grounds, I can't help but think of Sierra. She will be here today and it will be the first time we've seen each other since Vegas. It's only been a day; we left Vegas on Thursday evening and took Friday to recover before the wedding today but it feels like longer.

I realize with a start that I'm missing her.

I shake my head slightly, trying to shake the thoughts away. This is ridiculous. She's my assistant, nothing more. Yes, we had a moment of madness in Vegas, but that's all it was, all it can ever be. What happens in Vegas most definitely stays in Vegas in our case.

"Chance? Are you still with us?" Matt asks.

I turn back to face the room. Matt and I are dressed in our suits already.

Sebastian is putting the finishing touches to his, fastening his tie and tugging at it in front of the full length mirror.

"Yup, I'm here," I grin.

Sebastian turns to face us. "My tie's wonky," he says.

Matt laughs. "No it isn't," he insists.

"You wear a suit and tie literally every day," I say. "How can you be so concerned about that one?"

"Because this one is the only one that ever really mattered," he replies.

"Well, you have nothing to worry about. You look fine." I nod at him. "It's not even a little bit wonky." I pick up my half full glass of whiskey and hold it in the air. "To Sebastian," I say.

"To Sebastian," Matt repeats, holding his glass up.

Sebastian raises his glass and grins.

We all down our drinks and I move to fill our glasses up again. We still have a bit of time before we have to go downstairs and I think Sebastian's nerves are going to need all the help they can get if he's this worried about his tie.

"Okay, this has to be said," Matt says. "Does it strike either of you as weird that Sebastian, the man whore, is the first one of us to settle down and have kids and get married?"

He's not technically the first one to get married, but of course I can't say that. Instead. I laugh and nod my head. "Extremely," I say. "I always thought it would be you Matt."

"Well technically, Matt was the first one to actually settle down. He just hasn't gotten around to the wedding yet." Sebastian laughs. "Soon though huh, bro?"

Matt shrugs. "One day. For now, Callie and I are happy as we are."

I hand the drinks out and go back to the window with my own. I sit on the windowsill facing into the room.

"You know what would have been even weirder than this though?" Sebastian says.

"What?" Matt says.

Sebastian nods his head in my direction. "If Chance had gotten married first." He laughs.

"Chance's already married." Matt laughs.

My own laugh freezes on my lips. *He knows?* "Huh?" I manage to sputter out.

"To your job!" Matt laughs.

Relief floods me. Of course, he doesn't know. It's just a joke. A standard joke in our family that I should have recognized instantly. "Definitely the wife that causes the least amount of hassle." I smile.

Matt and Sebastian laugh.

"You're probably right there," Sebastian says.

"Your face when I said it though. It was as if you thought someone had somehow sneaked a marriage to you, without you knowing about it." Matt grins.

"No, horror is just my standard reaction to the M word." I laugh.

"Or any mention of any sort of relationship for that matter," Sebastian says. He nudges Matt. "Can you imagine a world where Chance finds a way to divide his time between work and a woman?"

"Not even a little bit." Matt grins.

"Me either to be honest," I add.

"You never know," Sebastian replies. "I always said I couldn't imagine a world where I could only ever have sex with the same person for the rest of my life. And when I finally let myself admit I loved Kimberley, I realized I never want to have sex with anyone else but her. Ever."

"Yeah. One day, you just might meet the one and realize the business won't implode if you leave the office before ten," Matt agrees.

I shrug and they raise their eyebrows. Normally I would completely dismiss the whole idea as ridiculous, but now I'm not so sure. I could imagine taking an evening off here and there if it meant I got to spend time with the side of Sierra I met in Vegas. But it's not going to happen. It would be the height of unprofessional.

"Relax." I grin. "I'm just humoring you both. There's no chance of it actually happening."

Matt and Sebastian both laugh.

Matt points at me. "You almost had me there. I thought maybe you and a certain someone who can't be named had found true love."

"We've been through this," I say.

"Yeah, yeah. Nothing happened. Nothing ever will. You don't see her that way. I know." Matt laughs. "But it's always fun to poke the bear and get a reaction."

He's right about getting a reaction. Sometimes it is fun. It's why we wind Sebastian up constantly. I wonder what reaction I'd get if I told them the truth about what Sierra and I did in Vegas. I wonder what reaction I'd get if I told them that even though an annulment is already underway, that not only have I not thrown my wedding ring away, but it's in my trouser pocket and it's been in one of my pockets since the second I slipped it off, outside of the hotel lobby.

A tap on the door pulls my attention away from the idea of dropping that bomb. Not that I was really considering it anyway.

"Come in," Sebastian calls.

Dad steps into the room and smiles proudly at Sebastian. "You look great son. Are you ready? You should be thinking of making your way down there now."

Sebastian nods slowly and swallows the rest of his drink.

My dad raises an eyebrow and smiles. "Nervous son?" he asks.

Sebastian shakes his head and then laughs. "Screw it. Yeah I'm terrified," he admits.

Dad claps him on the shoulder. "You'll be fine son. Trust me, I was a wreck on my wedding day. But once I saw your mom walking down the aisle towards me, all of the nerves melted away and I knew I was making the right choice."

Matt and I finish our drinks at a slightly slower pace as we listen.

"I'm not nervous about marrying Kimberley," Sebastian says. "I'm worried I'll stutter and splutter on the vows or mess something up."

"You won't," Dad says.

"Don't be so sure," Matt says with a wink. "He's likely to say the wrong name or something."

"Oh, thanks for that one. I hadn't even thought of that. And now, it's bound to happen." Sebastian sighs.

"Come on. Before these two talk you out of it." Dad laughs.

We leave the room and walk along a luxurious hallway. We take the elevator down to the ground floor and step out into the marble floored lobby. The whole lobby is decked out with white streamers and silver trim. We head out through the glass double doors to where the guests are gathering.

Dad shakes Sebastian's hand. "Good luck son. I'm proud of you. All three of you." He shakes my hand and Matt's hand and then he spots Mom in the crowd and makes his way towards her.

"Let's get you married," I say, clapping Sebastian on the back.

We begin to move through the crowd towards the front of the area where the officiant waits.

People see us and come over to congratulate Sebastian.

We stop walking for a moment while he chats to someone from the crowd.

Immediately, I scan the crowd and I try to tell myself I'm not looking for Sierra, but I know I am. My eyes are drawn to her instantly like she's the only person there.

She's sitting next to Bernie and a couple of the other girls from the office. She's wearing a pink, tight fitting gown that shows off her curves beautifully.

My cock twitches when I remember my hands on her hips and I will myself not to think about that now.

She looks tanned, glowing. Her hair is half up, pinned in little twirls and the bottom half hangs loose around her face. She must feel my eyes on her because she turns around and for a second, our eyes meet and I feel my stomach flip. She smiles and gives me a wave which I return. She turns back to the front, but not before I see the flush of pink creeping over her cheeks.

"Chance?"

"Hmm," I say.

Sebastian elbows me hard in the ribs. "Will you pay attention? Anyone would think it's you getting married!" He laughs.

"Sorry," I say. "I was just thinking about something."

"You're banned from thinking about work at my wedding. We've been over this."

"I know. I'm sorry. No more, I swear," I promise.

I'm just relieved he didn't realize where my gaze had fallen. I'd much rather him think I'm breaking his no work thoughts rule than believe I'm thinking about Sierra and how soft her skin is, how her hair feels like silk. I catch my attention wandering again and I force myself to stay in the present as we start moving again.

We reach the front of the area.

Matt and I are Sebastian's groomsmen, so we stay by his side as he nervously paces the altar area. "Have you turned your work phone off?" Matt asks me for the fourth time.

"Yes. Relax," I say. "Even I draw the line at taking calls in the middle of a wedding."

He laughs nervously and looks at his watch. "She's late," Sebastian says.

"Brides are always late. It's their thing," Matt tries to soothe him. "And it's only like two minutes."

I look out into the gathered guests again. I spot Callie sitting with my parents. Carl, Sebastian and Kimberley's son, sits on my mom's knee looking adorable in his tiny little suit. He looks content for now, but I can't help but wonder how long that's going to last. He's almost two now and two year olds don't take too kindly to being made to sit still when they don't want to.

I try to scan the room and pick out who is here and who isn't, but I'm fighting a losing battle. My eyes go straight back to Sierra and they stay there for a moment, fixed on her face. She looks up and smiles, her cheeks flushing slightly. I return her smile and quickly look away, sure I'm red and the whole congregation will be wondering why.

As quickly as I look away from her, my eyes go back to her.

She catches me looking again and this time, I hold her gaze until she's the one to look away first. She looks down into her lap, her cheeks on fire, biting her bottom lip.

God, I wish I was the one biting that lip.

I do look away then, knowing I can't start going down that road again, not up here. I glance back at my parents. My mom is looking back over her shoulder, straight at Sierra. She turns back to the front and catches my eye, giving me a wide, knowing smile.

I return her smile, trying to look casual. I need to find something else to focus on because if Mom has noticed where my attention is focused, then other people are going to start noticing too.

"Ladies and gentlemen, please rise for the bride," a voice calls from the other end of the aisle.

At least now, I have something else to concentrate on. Sebastian is getting married and I can focus all of my attention on the ceremony. The first chords of the *Bridal Chorus* rings out across the crowd as chairs scrape and feet clatter. The low hum of conversation dies down.

I glance at the piano behind the crowd. It's white and it fits the aesthetic of the wedding beautifully.

Kimberley appears at the end of the aisle, her two best friends either side of her. They fall back and pick up her train.

Kimberley has gone for a traditional white dress. The bodice is tight fitting, covered in diamantes and the skirt is looser. Her bump looks so cute in her dress. She looks absolutely beautiful. I mean not as beautiful as Sierra, but then who is?

She carries a bouquet of pink and white roses. Even through her veil, I can see her smiling, her eyes shining with happy tears as every eye in the room fixes on her. I hear Sebastian breathe a loud sigh of relief beside me and I look down at the ground for a second, so no one sees me almost laughing. As if Kimberley wasn't going to show. She's been in love with Sebastian since she was a kid.

She's almost at the arch when Carl spots her.

"Mommy pretty." He smiles, bouncing on my mom's knee.

His words get an aww from the crowd and a little giggle from Kimberley. She reaches the archway and her friends move to stand to one side, behind Kimberley, opposite from where Matt and I stand behind Sebastian. She hands the bouquet to one of the girls.

Sebastian is grinning like he's won the lottery and I think in some ways, he has. He bends down and kisses Kimberley's bump and then he straightens up and pushes her veil back. She beams at him and I can see the love radiating off her.

The officiant steps forward.

"Family and friends, we come together today to witness and celebrate the union of Sebastian Hunter and Kimberley Montgomery." He pauses for a moment and then goes on, "True marriage is more than simply joining two people together through the bonds of matrimony. It is also the union of two hearts and the blending of two families. It lives on the love you give each other and never grows old, but also thrives on the joy of each new day. Marriage is, and should be, an expression of love. May you always be able to talk things over, to confide in each other, to laugh with each other, to enjoy life together and to also share those moments of quiet and peace when the day is done. May you be blessed with happiness and a home of warmth and understanding."

I realize I have once more been staring at Sierra through the officiant's opening. Have we had a union of two hearts or did we just make a drunken mistake? I'm not so sure anymore, but I know it was more than just a whim. I think it happened because we were drunk, sure, but I think underneath it all was a genuine want for each other.

The officiant goes on as Sierra smiles at me again, a shy smile that makes my heart skip a beat. I give her a little smile back and then look away quickly. I can imagine her laughing on the inside at my discomfort.

"Do you, Kimberley Montgomery, take Sebastian Hunter to be your lawfully wedded husband. To have and to hold from this day forward, for better or for worse, for richer or for poorer, in sickness and in health, to love and to cherish from this day forward, until death do you part?"

"I do." Kimberley smiles. Tears shine in her eyes and one slips down her cheek. She reaches up and wipes it away without taking her eyes off Sebastian.

Suddenly, a thought hits me. One I never thought I would have. I want this. I want someone who looks at me the way Kimberley looks at Sebastian. I want someone who I love as completely as he loves her. I glance at Sierra again, pleased to discover she's already looking at me with a dreamy expression on her face. Maybe she's thinking the same thing as me.

I catch myself and shake my head ever so slightly, trying to dislodge my thoughts. It's just the occasion making me think silly things, that's all.

"Do you, Sebastian Hunter, take Kimberley Montgomery to be your lawfully wedded wife? To have and to hold from this day forward, for better or for worse, for richer or for poorer, in sickness and in health, to love and to cherish from this day forward, until death do you part?" the officiant goes on.

I hold my breath for a moment, sure Sebastian will take this moment to make some stupid joke or something, but of course he doesn't.

"I do," he replies without hesitation.

"And now the exchanging of the rings," the officiant says with a warm smile.

Matt digs in his pocket and pulls out the ring for Sebastian as one of the girls from Kimberley's side steps forward with the ring for her.

"Sebastian," the officiant prompts.

Sebastian takes the ring Matt is holding out and then he takes her hand in his.

Kimberley looks down at their joined hands for a moment and then her eyes go back to Sebastian's.

"Kimberley," Sebastian starts. "I give you this ring, as a symbol of my love for you, as I give to you all that I am and accept from you all that you are." He pushes the ring onto her finger.

"And now you, Kimberley," the officiant says.

Kimberley smiles and takes the ring from her maid of honor and then she takes Sebastian's hand in hers. Her voice is shaky with happy tears as she speaks, "Sebastian, I give you this ring, as a symbol of my love for you, as I give to you all that I am and accept from you all that you are." She smiles and pushes the ring onto his finger, her fingers lingering on his for a moment.

"I hereby pronounce you husband and wife. Sebastian, you may now kiss your bride."

Sebastian and Kimberley lean in to each other. Sebastian wraps his arms around Kimberley as they kiss.

The guests clap and cheer.

I glance at Sierra, wishing I could hold her in my arms like that and feel her lips on mine. She smiles up at me. I look away quickly, turning back to Sebastian and Kimberley with their long, lingering kiss.

Sebastian and Kimberley finally break their kiss and turn to face the guests.

"Ladies and gentleman, I present to you for the first time, Sebastian and Kimberley Hunter," the officiant announces.

This gets another round of applause. Sebastian takes Kimberley's hand in his and raises it above his head. The applause gets louder, with a few appreciative whoops and cheers thrown in.

I'm looking at Sierra again, and this time, I don't even bother trying to hide it. She stares back at me, her face glowing and happy. What I wouldn't give right now, to march over to her and take her in my arms and kiss her the way Sebastian has just kissed Kimberley.

The officiant comes over and asks Sebastian and Kimberley who will be their official witnesses and I focus my attention on that, knowing it won't be long until I'm looking at Sierra again. I think I can keep my attention focused on something other than her long enough to sign the register though. Or at least... I hope I can.

Chapter Thirteen

CHANCE

The time since the wedding ceremony has passed in a blur. After the register was signed and yes, I managed to stay focused on it long enough to get my signature in the right place, we moved to the area by the creek and had photographs taken and then we repeated the process close to some of the flower beds.

We went into the large dining area and had a sit down meal. Matt and I both gave speeches and Kimberley's maid of honor gave one too. Finally, Sebastian and Kimberley did their speeches and cut their cake.

We went back up to our rooms with a half hour to spare to get changed and freshen up for the evening. I'm kind of glad to be out of my suit. It's hot in the ballroom now, as the reception is well under way. I'm still wearing trousers and a dress shirt, but I've at least shed the jacket and the tie.

The DJ is playing good music and most of the room is up dancing. Kimberley and Sebastian had their first dance early and the dance floor has been full ever since.

I've spent most of the time here watching Sierra dancing, wishing I had the balls to go and ask her to dance with me. I kind of think she wants me to ask her. She keeps glancing over at me and smiling. But I just can't. I'm scared she'll say no and honestly, I'm scared she'll say yes and I end up stepping on her foot or something.

I search the dance floor looking for her again, but I can't see her. I scan the room and I catch sight of her pink gown. She's at the bar. She walks back to her table with a glass of wine. She's sitting alone and I know this is my chance. I might not be brave enough to ask her to dance, but surely I can talk to her. I mean I can't fuck that up quite as spectacularly as I could fuck up dancing with her.

I stand up and pick up my glass and head towards Sierra's table.

Looking up, she smiles as I approach.

I am taken by her shining eyes once more. "Hey, how are you?" I ask.

"I'm good thanks. You?" she replies.

"Good." I nod at the seat beside hers. "Mind if I join you?"

She shakes her head.

I sit down.

She smiles in the direction of Sebastian and Kimberley who are dancing and laughing in the middle of the dance floor. "They look so happy don't they?"

"They do." I nod. "They've been in love since they were teenagers. They lost touch for a while, but it was always meant to be with those two."

Sierra looks back at me, a teasing smile on her face. "Well, listen to you getting all romantic." She giggles.

I can't help but laugh along with her. *Am I really becoming a romantic? No, I'm just stating a fact surely.*

"I got a call from Sophie Miller yesterday," Sierra starts.

I reach out and gently put my finger on her lips, feeling that spark of energy flying between us the second my skin touches hers. "No work talk. Sebastian's rules." I grin and move my hand away.

She laughs. "Wow! You really are changing. Since when did you start to follow Sebastian's rules?"

"Well now, he's married, it'll be the last time he gets to put his foot down about anything. So, I'll give him his day." I laugh.

"Fair enough." Sierra laughs with me. "You know, that's got me thinking of something."

"What?" I ask.

She leans closer to me, whispering and I lean in to hear her. "Technically, we're still married right now. So does that mean I get to make the rules for now?"

"Not a chance." I grin.

"Shame," she says with a twinkle in her eye. "I had some really fun ideas too."

Oh I bet you did. And I bet I'd love to play along with any of them.

"Is that so?" I say, raising an eyebrow. "I don't think rules are meant to be fun."

"Ah well, you haven't heard mine, that's why," she replies. Her phone starts to ring in her handbag beside her. She smiles apologetically and pulls her phone out of her bag. "I have to take this," she says. "Would you excuse me for a moment?"

I nod, watching her walking away, her hips swaying inside of her dress.

She's still in ear shot when she answers her call. "Hi baby," she says.

Baby? Fucking baby?

I stand up so fast I almost knock the chair over. I've been taken for a complete and utter fool here. I'm not surprised Sierra was so willing to keep this whole wedding thing discrete. She clearly has a boyfriend. I can't believe I let myself imagine anything could happen between us again, however fleetingly. This is why I prefer working to dating. Work I understand. This is... well apparently, this is something that I'm totally horrible at.

I stalk back towards my table and sit down. I can't help but keep glancing at Sierra's table, even though I tell myself to get a grip.

She comes back after a few minutes. She looks around and spots me back at my table. She takes a step towards me, smiling.

I glare at her.

Her smile drops from her face and she sighs. She sits back down at her own table, her shoulders slumped.

I feel horrible for upsetting her like that, but I remind myself that I'm not the one with a secret partner here. She should be the one who feels horrible, not me. I can feel my temper rising and I remind myself this is Sebastian and Kimberley's day, their wedding, and I'm not going to ruin it by sitting here with a face like thunder. I can fake being happy for a few hours.

I finish my drink and head over to the bar for another one. As I return to my table, I keep my eyes fixed straight ahead, so I won't be tempted to look at Sierra.

My mom appears in my line of sight. She smiles and I return her smile, feeling some of the anger leaving me when I see how happy she is. She's glowing, the picture of a proud and happy mom.

She waits by my table until I reach it. I go to sit down and she shakes her head. "Don't think you're getting out of this one, Chance," she says.

"Out of what one?" I ask, genuinely puzzled.

"Out of dancing with your old mom." She grins.

The thought of dancing with mom is a whole lot less scary than the thought of dancing with Sierra was, and it will take my mind off her for a while. I smile at Mom and nod my head. I take a sip of my drink and put it down on the table. I offer Mom my arm and lead her out onto the dance floor. At least with her, I won't be a nervous wreck and stomp on her foot and fall over or something.

We reach a space on the dance floor and I twirl her around.

Mom takes my hands in hers. She leans in to talk to me as we sway to the music, "So, Sierra looks nice today doesn't she?" she says.

I can hear the laughter in her voice. She knows for a fact, I've noticed how good Sierra looks. I feel my body stiffen at the mention of her name, but still, my eyes seek her out over my mom's shoulder. She's still sitting at her table, but Bernie has joined her now and I feel glad that she's not sitting alone, even though she's hurt me. God, when did I get so fucking sappy? I need to go back to being myself. This wedding is having a strange effect on me and I don't like it one bit.

I can feel Mom's eyes searching my face and I realize her statement wasn't a rhetorical question. She's actually waiting for an answer, most likely because she wants to gauge my reaction.

"Yes," I reply.

"That's it? Yes," Mom asks.

I shrug. "You asked me a yes or no question. What else is there to say?" I reply, choosing my words carefully, knowing exactly where this conversation is going.

"The way you look at her has changed. Like you're noticing her for the first time. You like her don't you? As much more than just an assistant."

I can't deny it. Mom will see straight through it if I lie to her. And I'm certainly not about to tell her that Sierra and I got married and then I found out she has a boyfriend. I stick with the standard line, the one I know Mom will believe. "It doesn't matter how I look at her or how I see her. Dating Sierra would be highly unprofessional."

My mom laughs.

I frown at her, confused by her reaction.

She shakes her head and quickly rubs her hand over my cheek. "Ah Chance, you can't help who you fall for you know," she says.

"I haven't—"

"You have," she states firmly. "The fact that the only reason you can think of for not dating her is that it would be unprofessional confirms it."

I open my mouth to say something, anything that will convince her that she's wrong, but she's right. If I wasn't into Sierra, I would have just said that. Instead of trying to think of something else to say, something that no doubt will dig me deeper into this hole I've created and just make things worse. I end the conversation in a different way, spinning mom around quickly and making her laugh.

She's still twirling and laughing when the song ends. "Chance, you boys sure do keep me young, but right now, I'm feeling my age. My feet are killing me and I need a drink," she says.

I nod and start to follow her off the dance floor. I don't get far when Kimberley steps in front of me.

"Not so fast you." She grins. "You don't get to go to a wedding and get out of dancing with the bride."

I laugh as I offer her my hand and we dance. I still find my gaze wandering to Sierra, but it's different this time. No matter how long I stare at her, she isn't looking back at me anymore.

Chapter Fourteen

SIERRA

At the start of the day, I was really enjoying the wedding. The setting was beautiful. Kimberley and Sebastian make such a sweet couple. Throughout the ceremony, although I tried to concentrate on the vows and the officiant's words, I kept finding my gaze drawn to Chance. He looked so hot standing up there in his suit and now, I know what's beneath his suit and it just makes him all the more attractive.

Every time I looked at him, he was looking at me. The first few times our eyes met, he glanced away quickly, blushing and trying to make out like he wasn't looking at me. By the end of the wedding though, he was blatantly looking at me and I knew I could see the feelings I have for him on his face when our eyes met.

I began to believe that maybe we had a chance. That maybe what happened in Vegas wasn't a couple of days of crazy, but might actually be the start of something special. I was stupid to believe that obviously, but all of the signs were there, and it would have been next to impossible to read them as anything else.

His speech after the meal was warm and funny and I saw a glimpse of the man I had seen in Vegas. The man with more to him than just work. The man who could make me laugh without trying to. The man who deep down believed in true love, even if he would never admit it out loud.

As the evening reception got going, I hoped he would ask me to dance, but I told myself that really wasn't his style. There was no way he would allow his family to see him flirting and dancing with a girl. He's a private person and even when I was dancing with the girls and glancing at him every now again, feeling his eyes on me, I knew he wouldn't come to dance with me.

At the first opportunity, I slipped away from the girls, saying I needed a drink. I got my drink and instead of going back to the dance floor, I went back to my table, hoping he would come over. He did and we chatted and I found myself getting braver as we laughed. I hinted to Chance, no, more than hinted, I blatantly put it out there, that I was up for some fun. He seemed like he was lapping it up, playing along.

I went out of the room for a second to take a quick call and when I came back, he had gone back to his own table. I figured it was because he felt out of place sitting at my table alone and I took a step towards him, but the way he glared at me when I did told me it was much more than that. It told me he wasn't in the least bit interested in me now, since we were back to reality.

I had made a total fool of myself and the wedding was ruined for me. I knew I couldn't just leave straight away though. I didn't want him to think he'd had that much of an effect on me, so I painted on a fake smile, chatted to the girls and even had another dance.

It's getting close to midnight now and I know I can realistically leave without it looking suspicious. Other people have already started to leave. I finish the last of my drink and turn to Bernie. "Well, that's all for me."

"Oh, no way, Sierra. It's early yet. Stay a while," she says.

I shake my head.

"Go on, have one more drink," she coaxes me.

I'm really not enjoying being here and Chance is clearly avoiding me. It'll be best for us both if I just slink away. I shake my head. "I'm sorry, but it's been a long day and I'm tired."

"Your loss." Bernie laughs. "You'll miss Sebastian's robot dancing once he's really drunk."

I laugh and get up. "Another time maybe. Night," I say.

"Night," she says, waving after me.

I cross the dance floor, heading for the exit. I step off it onto the carpet and come face to face with Chance. He starts to turn away and I almost do the same, but then I think... no, fuck him. He doesn't just get to treat me this way. I think all of the wine is influencing my decision to force him to acknowledge me, but I don't care. If my flirting was making him uncomfortable, I would much rather him have just said that than play along and then ignore me.

I reach out and touch his arm, hating when I can feel my skin tingling where we touch, even though I'm so mad at him.

"I'm leaving," I announce and then cringe inside. This wasn't even close to how I imagined this conversation would start.

"Okay," Chance replies coolly. "I expect you in early on Monday, ready to make up for the slack from over the weekend."

"What happened to no work talk?" I snap.

He shrugs and goes to move past me.

I side step, standing in his way. "Is something wrong?" I ask.

He doesn't reply. He just stares at me with barely concealed anger.

I'm not sure how he gets to be the one who's angry here.

He goes to step around me again.

Again, I block his path. "No. You don't get to treat me this way. I don't appreciate your mood swings and I'm not a mind reader."

"What are you talking about?" he demands.

I almost walk away then. He's clearly playing dumb on purpose, but I decide I'm not going to give him the opportunity to think he's somehow, the wronged party here. "I'm talking about you blowing hot and cold on me for no apparent reason. One minute, we were having a laugh, and don't try to tell me you weren't flirting with me because I won't believe it. And then the next minute, you were looking at me like you can't stand the sight of me. What was it? Did I make you uncomfortable having a laugh with you? Or are you so full of yourself you're offended because I took a phone call while we were talking?"

"Let's just say my mood swings are linked to whether or not a person deceives me," he says.

Okay, now I'm lost.

My utter confusion must show on my face because Chance rolls his eyes and shakes his head. "Okay, I'll spell it out for you. It would have been nice if you had told me you were in a relationship before we had sex. I'm not the kind of guy that gets involved in drama like that Sierra and you of all people know that about me."

I barely register what he's saying after the part about me being in a relationship. *What the hell is going on here?* "Okay, back up a step or two there," I say. "I have no idea what you're talking about."

"I'm talking about the 'hi baby' phone call," he snaps. "You should have told me Sierra, not have me find out by over hearing something like that."

I can't help it. As I realize what he's referring to, I throw my head back and laugh.

Chapter Fifteen

CHANCE

I've spent the entire night after talking to Sierra, trying my best to avoid her. I've done well at it too... until now. I had just been to the bathroom and as I came back into the ballroom, she was heading for the exit. I looked away quickly when I saw it was her, but she wasn't having any of that.

She seems to want to drag the whole thing out and make it even more painful. I finally told her I know about her boyfriend after trying to get away from her a few times. At first, she tried to play it like she didn't know what I was talking about, but now, she's actually fucking laughing at me.

Maybe being faithful doesn't mean much to her, but it does to me. I know I'm not exactly Mr. Warm and Fuzzy Relationship Guy, but I believe a relationship is between two people. I don't want any part of anything that involves one of those people being cheated on.

I shake my head in disgust at Sierra. How could she be so fucking callous? I mean fair enough, we had a fling, so if she wants to laugh at me, then whatever. But her poor boyfriend is the one she's really making a fool out of.

I go to walk away and once more, she stops me, putting her hand on my arm.

I ignore the way her fingers make my skin tingle and try to shake her off, but she keeps her grip and waits until I'm looking at her face.

She's stopped laughing now. "I'm sorry for laughing, but this is all just a big misunderstanding," she says.

"Oh really?" I'm sceptical, but I want it to be a misunderstanding so badly that I wait for her explanation.

"The phone call I got was from my niece. She's staying with my parents for the night."

I feel a mix of emotions slam through me. Relief that Sierra isn't taken. Ashamed that I misjudged the situation and her so badly without even asking her to explain, and the surety that I've fucked up any chance of anything happening between us. "I'm so sorry, Sierra," I say, putting my hand over hers for a moment where it still rests on my arm. "I should have spoken to you about it, instead of acting like a douchebag. I was just... I was hurt."

The hard expression in her eyes starts to fade when I tell her I was hurt.

I know if I have any chance of fixing this, I have to act now. "Can I buy you a drink to say sorry? Just one before you go?" I say.

She debates it for a second while I silently will her to put me out of my misery.

"Okay." She smiles.

Relief floods me and I take her to the bar. I get her a glass of white wine and get a brandy and coke for myself. Then I lead Sierra to one of the quieter tables lining the room.

Everyone is still dancing and having fun and no one is paying the slightest bit of attention to us.

"I'm sorry," I say again, as we sit down.

"It's all right," she says.

It's not though. Not really. I've just shown her that I'm a jealous idiot. *Wonderful.* God, I should have just asked her to dance and trodden on her damned foot. It wouldn't have been anywhere near as embarrassing as this is.

"You know, I never even considered you might think that was anyone other than my niece I was talking to," she explains. "I should have really though, because this is all still so new. My sister passed away five months ago, she had a brain tumor, and her daughter, my niece, has come to live with me now."

Once more, she shames me. I have known this woman for two years, she's been right by my side through thick and thin at work, and up until now, I didn't even know she had a sister, let alone that she'd lost one. I've fucked up enough tonight by not just being honest. "I'm so sorry," I say softly. "I honestly didn't even know you had a sister. Let alone that she was sick."

"You didn't?" she asks, surprised. "I always assumed your other assistant had told you about my sister passing away and that you just felt awkward mentioning it."

I shake my head. "No. I mean I'm hardly warm and fuzzy but I would have at the very least offered you my condolences and some time off."

"I took some time off for the funeral. Remember, I asked for three days off earlier in the year? You said yes without asking any questions and that's why I figured you knew."

I shake my head again. "I remember you asking for the time off. I didn't know why, but I knew it must be important because you've never asked for time off in all of the time you've worked for me. How are you managing to look after your niece and not need time off now? We can work something out you know."

"I'm the nearest thing that girl has to a mom now Chance, but I'm still a career woman. I don't feel the need to take time off work because I have a child with me. She's got school and then she goes to my parents' house for a few hours. If anything, having her come to live with me has made me more determined to be successful; I want to make a good future for her, and that means putting the hours in."

I nod my head, feeling selfish that part of me is relieved Sierra isn't going to go part time or anything. She is the best assistant I have and I don't know what I'd do without her. "Tell me about her," I prompt. "Your niece I mean."

"Her name is Hayley. She's seven going on seventy." Sierra grins. "She tests my patience almost every day and she's full of a thousand and one questions, most of which I don't have the answers to. But she's funny, bubbly and full of confidence, and I wouldn't change her for the world."

"She sounds like quite a character." I laugh.

"Oh, she is." She beams at me. "She gets her stubborn streak from her mom, but the temper on her? Holy shit, she has a short fuse, and if she thinks something is unjust, she isn't shy about making it known. She definitely gets that from her father."

"I don't know about that," I say, returning her smile. "Maybe she gets that from her aunt."

"Oh, no way, I'm not taking the blame for that one." She laughs.

"So what happened to Hayley's father? Was he married to your sister at some point?" I ask, curious as to why Hayley is living with Sierra and not him.

"Oh, God no." Sierra shakes her head while wincing at the idea. "Hayley was my sister's world and she wouldn't ever wish she didn't have her, and that's the only reason she didn't wish she had never met Hayley's father. To say, he was a mistake would be an understatement up there with saying the sun won't burn you."

"I take it he doesn't see much of Hayley then?" I ask.

"He's seen her the grand total of twice. Once the day after she was born and the other time on her second birthday. He has no interest in being a father and I have no interest in Hayley growing up thinking there's something wrong with her because her dad is an irresponsible jerk who can't make time for his daughter. After my sister died, there was talk of contacting him, seeing if he would man up and be a father to Hayley, but I put my foot down and said no. My sister and I had talked about it, and I had promised her when the time came, Hayley would be coming to live with me, and it's a promise I intended to keep." Her eyes flash with fire and then she shakes her head. "I'm sorry. I didn't mean that to come out sounding quite so bitter." She sighs.

"Not at all. I understand," I say. "But let me tell you something. If he is too stupid to see what he's missing out on, then it's him that has something wrong with him. Because if Hayley is even a tiny bit as amazing as you are, then she's a very special girl indeed."

Sierra looks down at the table, blushing and smiling. She looks back up. She's serious again, but her eyes still gaze into mine. "I only wish he saw it that way. But I've made my peace with it, and I'm not bothered for myself. I'm happy never to see him again. I love having Hayley with me and I don't need anything from him. It's her, I'm bothered for. She's just getting to that age where she keeps asking me why her friends all have dads and she doesn't."

"That must be hard," I say. "What do you tell her?"

"I tell her I'm awesome enough that she doesn't need him." Sierra laughs. "But sooner or later, that's not going to wash anymore and I'll have to tell her the truth."

"It sounds to me like you're already telling her the truth." I smile.

She blushes again and picks up her drink. She finishes it in one long swallow.

I know I said one drink, but I really don't want her to leave. I feel like we're really connecting. We're not talking about work and we're not just having hot sex. We're connecting as people. I know this is dangerous ground. As much as I like

Sierra, and as much as I crave being with her, I can't start screwing around with my assistant. It would be one thing to ease up off work a little and start dating, but dating someone who works so closely with me is more than easing up a little. It would be taking my eye off the ball completely and I can't do that.

"Another drink?" I say, even as I convince myself this is a bad idea.

"One more." Sierra smiles.

I go to the bar and get another round and head back to the table. Even now, I can't believe I have never seen Sierra as the warm and genuinely funny person she is before this last week. I can't believe I didn't see how attractive she is. I really am an idiot.

Sierra raises her glass.

I clink mine against it.

She takes a drink and sets the glass down on the table. "Have you ever wanted children?"

I shrug. "I've never really thought about it. I don't hate children or anything, and I mean *never say never* and all that, but as I think you know, I've always been more focused on work than thinking about starting a family or anything like that."

She giggles and nods rapidly.

I frown.

"Sorry," she says. "I just got this vision in my head of you behind your desk with a toddler on your lap, telling him how to run your empire."

"That's not funny. It's exactly how it would go." I grin.

"That's why it's so funny," she says. "Because I can actually picture it."

She stops laughing and takes another sip of wine. "Seriously though, do you ever picture yourself taking a step back from work and settling down in the future?"

"Honestly, up until today, no," I say. "But when I saw Kimberley and Sebastian exchanging their vows and I saw how happy they made each other, I kind of changed my mind. I felt myself wanting that kind of love."

"Yeah, they really do have something special don't they?"

I nod and laugh. "Yeah. It's sickening isn't it?"

Sierra laughs and gently slaps my arm. "Stop it! They're cute together."

"Yeah, I guess," I say. "Seriously, I'm happy for them, really. Sebastian isn't so bad and he deserves to be happy."

"Yeah and if he starts slacking off after baby number two comes along, it gives you more of an excuse to work more," Sierra adds.

I shudder and shake my head. "God no. Sebastian's job is too focused on numbers. Bottom lines, profit and loss, taxes. All of that shit bores me to tears. Now, if one of my designers decided to have a baby and start slacking off, well I'd have to sack him." I laugh at Sierra's shocked expression. "I'm joking," I say. "I'd be happy to pick up the extra work in that department is what I meant."

"Sometimes, I'm surprised you don't make them all go part time, so you can spend more time at the office."

"That's actually a good idea." I grin.

Sierra laughs. "The worst thing about that is I reckon you mean it."

"Oh, I do," I say. "Anyway, we're breaking Sebastian's rules again. No more work talk."

"Deal." She looks at me with a twinkle in her eye. "We could dance instead."

I think about it for a moment, the fear of being clumsy grabbing me again. I tell myself to get over it and then I look to my left. Double doors open onto a patio. I stand up and hold my hand out to Sierra.

Her eyes open wide with shock, she clearly was expecting me to say no, but she slips her hand into mine and lets me help her to her feet.

I lead her away from the dance floor, towards the double doors.

"Ummm, I think we're going the wrong way." She laughs. "We..." Her words die in her throat when we step out onto the patio.

The furniture has been pushed to one side and fairy lights hang all over the wooden rafters above us. More twirl around the columns that stand on either side of the patio, holding the rafters in place. The music is softer out here, but we can still hear it. The patio is deserted as I had hoped it would be.

"Are you sure about that?" I ask her with a smile.

"Nope. Seems you were going the right way all along."

I step towards her and pull her into my arms. She wraps her arms around my waist and rests her head on my shoulder and we begin to sway gently to the music. Having her in my arms again, pushes away all of my misgivings about anything happening between us. All I can think about is how good it would feel to kiss her right now.

She's humming to the music, just loud enough for me to hear her and I can't help but smile at her tuneless noise.

As the song ends, she lifts her head up from my shoulder and looks at me.

We stop swaying, but neither of us makes any move to release our hold on each other.

I feel my head leaning down, my body responding to the closeness of her, even though my mind is telling me no. As our lips touch, there's no question of this being a no.

I want her. I want her badly.

Surely, tonight can be an extension of Vegas. It's not like we're back at work and it is a wedding. I mean it's a special occasion, a special circumstance, so we're allowed to let our hair down and have one more crazy night.

Sierra's tongue wrapping around mine tells me she's thinking the exact same thing. So, I force myself to stop thinking at all and just enjoy the moment here with her. My cock is responding to her body pressed tightly against mine. It's straining against my zipper, trying to break free of its confines and get to her. I know she can feel it against her because she keeps rubbing herself against it, sending waves of pleasure and need through me.

When I can't stand it any longer, I pull away from her.

We stand panting, looking at each other.

I can see the lust all over Sierra's face. "Do you want to get out of here?"

"I thought you'd never ask." She grins at me.

Chapter Sixteen

CHANCE

We reach the door to my room and I honestly don't know how I've kept my hands off Sierra all the way up here. Well, it hasn't been all of the way up here. We kissed in the elevator— a passionate, desperate kiss of two people who know this will be the last time they can be together— and want to savor every second of the time they have left.

I can't wait to get her into my room and devour her. I fumble in my pocket for my key card. I can't find it.

Sierra really isn't helping matters. She has wrapped her arms around my waist from behind. She leans closer to me, kissing my neck, sending shivers of pleasure through me, and her hands have already made their way beneath my shirt. They're moving lower.

"Sierra, stop!" I laugh.

"Are you sure?" she teases me.

My hand finally closes on the key card to pull it out and slip it into the slot. "Nope, keep going." I step into the room, flick on the light, and turn to Sierra. I wrap my arms around her waist, lifting her up.

She wraps her legs around me, her arms around my neck and our lips meet again. I kick the door closed behind me as I walk her further into the room. Her dress is around her hips where she pushed it up to wrap her legs around me and I run one hand down her bare thigh.

I move towards the wall and press Sierra against it, kissing her like I've been unleashed. My tongue is wrapped around hers, my hands are all over her, on her thighs, on her waist, in her hair. Her hands roam beneath my shirt, running all over my skin.

I move my mouth from hers to kiss down her neck and over one bare shoulder.

She shivers in my arms and moans as I run my tongue along her collarbone. "Chance," she whispers.

Her voice somehow pulls me out of the spell that has been cast over us, and I come back to my senses. I kiss her hard on the mouth again, and then I set her down on the ground. "This is a terrible idea."

"I know," she agrees, taking hold of my shirt and pulling me back towards her.

We kiss again, a frantic, passionate kiss that sets my soul on fire.

"We shouldn't," I mumble into her mouth.

"I know," she says again as she's unbuttoning my shirt. She gets it open and pushes it down my arms.

I step back again, trying and failing to resist her touch. "Sierra, listen. We both know this is it. This is all we can ever be. We can't be together. It would be unprofessional."

"I agree." She pushes me backwards until my legs hit the bed and I fall into a sitting position. She presses on my shoulders, forcing me backwards until I'm half laying down, then she straddles me and runs her tongue over my bare chest.

Her licking sends shivers through my whole body and my cock is screaming to be in her pussy, but I need to know she understands that I can't give her more than this. "Sierra," I whisper, almost pleadingly.

Finally, she stops driving me wild and sits up straight. She looks me in the eye. "I get it. You're not using me, Chance. I want this as much as you do and like you, I don't want some tacky office romance. We've got tonight and then we're done. Think of it like an extension of Vegas."

Her words spur me on. "Are you sure?"

She nods her head. "Yes. Are you trying to talk me out of this?"

"No." I grin. "I'm just making sure you're really up for what's coming next."

"And what's that?" she asks playfully.

I sit up and kiss her then I gently push her back onto her feet.

She frowns at me.

I grin. "Strip for me," I breathe the order out.

Her eyes widen for a second.

I think I've pushed her too far.

Then she bites her bottom lip and the look in her eyes is pure lust. She takes a few steps back from me and kicks off her shoes.

I match her, taking off my own shoes and socks.

She runs her hands over the silky material of her dress, moaning softly as her hands skim her body.

I jump up long enough to take off my pants and my boxers, then I sit back down to enjoy the show, glad my cock is finally free of its restraints.

Sierra grins at me and reaches behind herself. She pulls her zipper down and her dress falls to the ground. She kicks it to one side. She stands before me in a pair of pale pink panties, a silver necklace and nothing else.

I feel my heart racing, my temperature soaring off the scale. I stand up and take a step towards her.

She shakes her head. "Sit."

I am a little shocked, but I find myself following her order, turned on by her commanding tone.

"You can look, but you can't touch," she teases me. She runs her tongue over her finger tips.

I imagine the roughness of her tongue and the smoothness of her lips, and how they would feel on my cock. I swallow hard as she takes her nipples in her moistened fingers and begins to work them. She puts her head back, giving me a perfect view of her show.

I can hardly breathe watching her and the breaths I do manage to snatch are ragged and painful, but I don't care. All I care about is her. I want so badly to grab her and fuck her raw, but I don't want to miss this. She's so fucking hot, so fucking sexy, and she's doing all of this for me.

She's moaning now, her fingers working faster. She tugs on her nipples, stretching her breasts out and moaning again. She moves her hands lower, rubbing them over her stomach and hips. She hooks her thumbs into the waistband of her panties and pushes them down, kicking them away to join her discarded gown.

"Do you want to see more?" she asks me in a low, husky voice dripping with sex.

"Yes," I reply, barely able to get the word out.

"Do you want me to touch myself for you?"

I nod, unable to find my voice for a second.

Smiling with her hands resting on her stomach, she teases me with their proximity to her pussy, but not moving any closer. "Tell me," she says. "Tell me what you want."

I want to fuck her, but I want this to last. I find my voice, not willing to risk missing out on this, "I want you to play with yourself until you come for me," I say.

She smiles and reaches between her legs with one hand.

I moan with her as her fingers start to work her clit. I can hear how wet she is as she moves her fingers and I want to touch her, to taste her, to drink in her juices. I resist the urge to go to her, knowing instinctively she'll let me know when she's ready for my touch.

As her fingers move, her breathing gets more ragged, and her hot gaze on me gets more intense. If I can't touch her, I want to at least touch myself. This is agony. Torture. Exquisite, beautiful torment. I reach down to jerk off, but I know if I touch my cock now, I'll come and I don't want to come yet. I have all night to come, to do it over and over again, and right now, I just want to focus on the way Sierra is moving her hand so fast, it's almost a blur. I want to focus on the vein that's pulsing in her neck as she throws her head back, showing me she's as turned on as I am.

"Chance," she moans, drawing out my name, as she comes hard. She gasps, her body frozen for a moment. Her hand stops working her clit, moving back up over her stomach as her orgasm blasts through her body. She holds herself still, enjoying the sensation, her mouth hanging open as she moans again. Her eyes are half closed, her lips red and swollen. Her fingers are so wet they glisten.

Her eyes come fully open and she smiles at me, the smile of a vixen. She steps closer. "No touching," she reminds me.

"Yes, ma'am," I say, transfixed by her sensual body.

She is standing so close now, that I could grab her and kiss her, and I know if I did, she would let me, but that would mean this would be over—and this is by far, the hottest thing I have ever fucking seen in my life.

She takes her still wet fingers and runs them over my lips. I can smell her juices on her fingers. She moves her hand and I feel the wet, sticky coating she's left behind on me.

"Taste me. Taste what you do to my body," she purrs.

I don't need telling twice. I run my tongue over my lips, tasting her pleasure. The taste almost pushes me over the edge and I have to bite down on my lip to stop myself from climaxing.

Sierra watches me, an amused smile on her lips. She knows exactly what she's doing to me and she's loving it.

So am I.

"Do I taste good?" she asks.

I nod, not trusting my voice not to fail me.

She lifts her hand to her own mouth and sucks on her fingers, one by one, lapping her tongue all around them. She smiles at me when she's done. "You're right. I do taste good. But I bet you taste better."

She gets to her knees in front of me and pushes my legs apart, crawling in between them. She runs her tongue up the length of my cock.

I hear myself making an *aah* noise as pleasure explodes through me.

She licks over the tip of me, tasting my pre-cum. She makes an mmm sound and pulls back slightly. "I was right. You taste amazing," she whispers.

Her breath tickles the insides of my thighs, sending tingles through my whole body. She leans back down to me and sucks my cock into her mouth. Her lips are soft but firm and the way she rubs them up and down me makes me moan as ecstasy explodes through me. Her warm tongue laps at me, licking and tasting me and she keeps making an mmm sound, like she's enjoying the way I taste.

I can't hold back from touching her for even a second longer, so I reach down and push my hands into her hair. The clips that were holding her hair in place are long gone already, lost in the heat of the moment.

She sucks me hard and my hands ball into involuntary fists in her hair as fire floods through my body. I pull on her hair, unable to stop myself and she makes a hissing sound as she gasps in surprise, but the tugging seems to spur her on, her head moving faster and faster, her mouth frantic on me.

I can't hold myself back any longer and I let myself relax, my climax flooding through me, slamming through my cock and up through my stomach. I gasp in a breath and let it out in a long, low moan that turns into an almost animal sound, a primal growl filled with lust.

I feel my release coming and I spurt, my cock pulsing wildly as I come in Sierra's mouth. She continues to suck me, swallowing my cum and pulling out more, milking me dry with her swollen lips. She sucks and sucks, drinking down every last drop like it's the most wonderful thing she's ever tasted.

My climax begins to fade and I pant desperately, trying and failing to get myself back under control. I don't know how Sierra has this effect on me, it's like my cock has been waiting for her every bit as much as my heart has.

Sierra gets to her feet and stands looking down at me. She gives me a half smile and runs her tongue over her lips. She reaches up and wipes her finger along the outside of her bottom lip, where a tiny drop of my cum has dribbled from her mouth. She licks her finger.

I feel my body pulsing again, ready for her once more. "God, you're beautiful..." I get to my feet, cup her face in my hands and kiss her.

Her arms wrap around me, her hands roaming over my back, pinching, caressing, like she wants to touch every part of me at once. Her touch has an almost desperate quality to it. She wants this as much as I do.

I walk her towards the wall as I kiss her. I press her up against it and then I move my lips from hers, kissing down along her neck, her chest and over her breasts. I get to my knees before her. "Your turn." I grin up at her.

I take one of her legs and wrap it around my shoulder and then I reach for the other one. She lets me lift her off her feet, settling her leg over my shoulder. I press her back against the wall, pinning her in place, my palms either side of her ass, and then my tongue finds her clit and she moans loudly.

I work her clit until she's almost at the point of climaxing and then I move my tongue back through her lips and to her pussy. I push my tongue inside of her, finding her g-spot, pressing my tongue down on it.

She moans again and begins to move her hips, writhing herself against my face.

I move back slightly and cup her ass, gently lowering her down the wall until she's sitting on the ground. I'm going to make her come so hard she forgets who she is—where she is, and I don't want her to fall.

Her legs are still clamped around my shoulders while my tongue is still working her G-spot. I stretch my legs out behind me, laying down on my front, working her relentlessly. She calls out my name as her orgasm hits her. Her pussy tightens, clenching around my tongue as my face is bathed in a glorious slick of her juices.

I put my hands against her inner thighs and push them apart hard. She releases her clamp like hold on my shoulders and I pull my head back for a moment, my tongue slipping out of her pussy. I spread her legs wider, looking down at her glistening slit. I get to my knees between her legs and I run my fingers across her swollen red lips and find her clit again. I work my fingers side to side, making Sierra gasp.

Her next orgasm hits her before her first one is quite finished and her body goes rigid, her muscles tightening as pleasure assaults her.

I keep working her, feeling her clit pulsing against my fingers as wave after wave of pleasure goes through her entire body. She's whimpering now, her head rolling from side to side as her body responds to my touch.

Her whimper becomes a drawn out scream of my name and I feel heat flood my own body at the sound of my name on her lips. I pull my fingers away from her clit and lean forward. I kiss her stomach and then run my tongue down along it, moving over her mound and back to her clit again. I tease her, licking gently and slowly across her clit. She lifts her hips up, pressing herself against my tongue.

I move back out of her reach and gently blow on her swollen clit. I lean closer to flick my tongue over her then I suck it into my mouth, rubbing it between my tongue and the roof of my mouth.

Sierra cries out, a sound full of lust and want and need.

I massage her clit against the roof of my mouth until I feel her tense up again and another orgasm explodes through her body.

I can't wait any longer. I need to be inside of her tight, hot pussy. I need to fuck her like I've never fucked anyone before. My cock is ready, standing to attention, pulsing with need. I wait for Sierra's body to relax and then I lean forward and kiss her mouth. She rubs her tongue against mine and then licks over my lips, tasting herself on me.

I pull back and grasp her by the shoulders. I roll her onto her front.

Knowing what's coming, she gets onto all fours and then puts her palms against the wall. She looks at me over her shoulder and nibbles on her lower lip. "Fuck me," she says in a husky voice dripping with her need for me.

My cock pulses at her words and I move closer to her, running my cock through her lips, spreading her juices around. She's so fucking wet and just knowing I have done that to her makes my insides burn with pleasure.

I push my cock into her and take hold of her hips. I begin to move, losing myself in Sierra's pussy, feeling her clamping around me like a warm, tight glove. I start off slowly with long almost lazy thrusts that fill her right up. I want her to feel every inch of me inside of her and I want to claim every inch of her pussy as mine.

The feel of her slick pussy drives me mad and I soon find that I'm speeding up, not able to hold myself back from Sierra at all. I pull her hips back, meeting my thrusts and when I move one hand, Sierra keeps up the rhythm. I move my hand around to the front of her body and pinch one of her nipples in my fingers. Her head flies up, her breath coming in a startled hiss. Her nipple is rock hard and as I continue to pinch it in my fingers and stretch it out, she moans my name.

I work her nipple for a few seconds and then I release it and run my fingers down her spine. Her back arches, her skin coming out in a rush of goosebumps where I touch her. I move my hand over her ass cheek and around to the front of her body again, and push my fingers inside of her lips, pressing on her clit in time to my thrusts.

Sierra gasps in a strangled breath and then I feel her pussy tighten around me. Her orgasm is so intense that for a moment, her walls pin my cock in place and I can't move. It relaxes slightly and I slam myself all the way into her, making her cry out.

Beads of sweat coat her back and she lifts her head up as she comes hard, soaking my cock in her juices. Her arms are shaking and I don't think she's going to be able to brace herself against the wall much longer. I wrap my arm around her waist and pull her body back against mine and then I up my thrusts, slamming into her fast.

She is a wreck, whimpering and moaning and I can feel her orgasm ripping through her as her muscles clamp once again around my cock. A shudder of pleasure runs through her whole body and she makes a contented sighing noise.

My own orgasm is upon me now, holding me in its vice of pleasure and I feel my cock go wild, pulsing and spurting into her. My stomach is on fire, heat radiating out to my limbs, every nerve ending in my body feeling my orgasm washing through me, carrying me away to a place where there is nothing but sexual bliss.

I close my eyes and I feel like I'm floating on a soft wave as my climax holds me in its throes. I press my face against the warm skin of Sierra's neck, nuzzling against her while saying her name into her neck.

My arms and legs are turning to jelly as my orgasm recedes, my chest is heaving, my heart racing.

Sierra sits back on my legs, clutching the arm I have wrapped around her waist. She too, is gasping for breath and I can feel her body shaking slightly against mine. I tighten my grip on her waist and we stay that way for a moment, getting ourselves back under control. I can feel liquid running out of Sierra's pussy, coating my thighs, a mixture of her juices and mine.

The air around me smells of sex; musky and exotic, filled with wanton lust and pheromones. It's a primal smell, the smell of two bodies becoming one, and the scent makes my cock start to harden again.

Sierra shifts against me, rubbing her ass over my cock. She laughs softly. "You're ready again?" she says, sounding surprised.

"Sierra, when it comes to you, I'll never not be ready," I whisper into her hair.

Chapter Seventeen

SIERRA

*a*s Chance tells me he'll never not be ready for me, my heart skips a beat. I know it's only his hormones talking, the testosterone that's surging in his body... the lust and the closeness of the moment, but I can't help but wonder if he means it. Like *really* means it.

It doesn't matter though. Tonight is all this can ever be. Chance made it clear to me before we did this that once we're back at work on Monday, this can never happen again. And I know he's right. I don't want to be *that* woman—the one who is sleeping with her boss. But it won't make letting him go any easier. I have to though.

But not yet. Because tomorrow is another day and I intend to make the most of tonight. I turn in Chance's arms, hooking my legs on either side of his. I wrap my arms around his neck to lean in and kiss him.

He tastes of me, of my lust for him. Tasting my juices on his tongue sends shivers through me. I lick over his lips, wanting to taste every part of him, every drop of me on him. I push my tongue back into his mouth, moving my hands up into his hair and pressing us more tightly together. His hands rest on my hips and as our kiss deepens, they begin to roam, moving up my sides and then down my back.

His touch sends sparks through my skin. It feels like a melting heat if taking over my entire body. Then goosebumps fly over my skin, bringing with them a wash of excitement, a longing for him to fuck me again. I can't get enough of him. We may only have tonight, but if we had forever, I still don't think I could get enough of his touch, of the scent of him, the taste of him. He has consumed me, made me his. Made me want him in a way I didn't think I could ever want anyone.

I move one of my hands from his hair, running it along the side of his face and down his neck. I trail my nails lightly down his chest, pulling my body back slightly to give me room to touch him.

He tightens his grip on me, keeping me from falling backwards off his lap.

I run my nails down his stomach and keep moving lower until my hand brushes against his cock and he moans into my mouth. I wrap my hand around his cock, feeling the hardness of it, feeling every vein beneath his skin. I move my hand up and down and he moans again, louder this time.

"Fuck, you're amazing," he mumbles, moving his mouth down my neck, kissing along my shoulder as I work him.

I keep moving my hand, my grip firm. I start to speed up, enjoying the way his breathing becomes ragged. Knowing that I have this kind of power over him – I can make a man like Chance come completely undone at the seams – turns me on so much I feel a rush of wetness running from my pussy. As my juices coat Chance's thighs, he moans again.

I jerk him off for a few more minutes, until his breathing becomes so ragged, so fast, that I know I have to stop or he's going to come. I release my grip on him.

His eyes fly open. They're glassy, lust filled, and he holds my gaze for a second, stroking my hair back from my face, and then our mouths are on each other again, a frantic kiss that tells me how much we both need this.

I lift my ass slightly, still kissing him and reach down to take his cock in my hand again. I position myself over it and lower myself back down, impaling myself on his cock. It's so big that even now, even when I'm this turned on and this wet... I can feel him stretching me. It's a delicious feeling, a slight sting and a sensation of my body opening itself up to Chance, taking him into me.

I put my hands on his shoulders, pull back from his kiss as I move up and down on him. I look deeply into his eyes as I move, using his shoulders to lever myself up and down on him, wanting all of him inside of me.

His hands move up and down my back as his hips thrust, matching my movements. We are one, moving as one, feeling as one. Warmth builds in the center of me, spreading out, filling all of my body with pleasure.

Chance moves his hands to cup my ass and he lifts me, getting to his feet with his cock still inside of me, holding me up like I am weightless. I clamp my legs around his waist, bouncing furiously up and down on him as my climax starts to build. I need the release only he can bring me. I need to feel the pleasure cascading through me, filling me with Chance.

He walks me to the wall and slams my body against it and then he goes to town on my neck; his lips, his tongue, even his teeth, working my skin and sending tingles through me. I can feel him in every part of me. My skin is like one giant nerve ending.

I can feel my orgasm thundering closer and as my release comes, I lose myself for a moment. I feel my eyes rolling back in my head, and my vision is nothing but a red, pulsing dot of lust. Sheer ecstasy flows through my veins in place of blood and I am no longer breathing. I don't need oxygen; I need Chance's touch.

My orgasm pins me in place against the wall as my vision slowly returns and I find myself once more looking deeply into Chance's eyes. I see my own thoughts, my own pleasure, written all over his face, like he's feeling everything I'm feeling.

I feel my pussy twitch slightly, an after effect of the huge orgasm that is now starting to fade. Chance thrusts faster, his own climax coming now. I clench my pussy, tightening myself around him, pulling him in deeper. He moans and brushes his lips lightly against mine, and then he's coming. I can feel the warmth of his cum filling me up. He buries his face against my neck as his back tightens and his body goes hard against mine. I cling to him, my fingers digging into his shoulders as he spurts again, and then he relaxes, panting against my neck, his breath sending tingles through me all over again.

He pulls me away from the wall.

I know if he puts me down, my legs won't hold me. My knees will buckle and I'll tumble to the ground, but I know Chance won't let me fall.

He doesn't. He keeps me held tightly against him as he walks to the bed. He reaches down with one hand and pulls the duvet back and then he lays me down gently. He pulls the duvet over me and walks around to the other side of the bed.

I roll over, so I'm facing him as he goes to get in.

He gets into the bed beside me and leans forward and brushes his lips over mine again. "That was amazing," he says quietly.

"You were amazing." I smile.

He puts his arm around my waist, pulling me closer and I snuggle against him, putting my arm around his waist. We lay that way, looking into each other's eyes, searching each other's faces.

My limbs are like jelly and my body feels heavier than it should, but it's a nice sort of heavy. The sort that makes you want to close your eyes and float away on a cloud. I let my eyes close for a moment and then I open them again. I don't want to fall asleep. Not yet. I want to make the most of the time we have together.

Chance's eyes are closed and he's breathing deep and even.

I guess I wore him out I think to myself with a smile. I lean in and kiss him gently on the lips.

He mumbles something I can't make out and pulls me closer.

I watch him sleep for a few minutes, wanting to remember this moment, to remember what he looks like when he lets his softer side show. I know this is the last time we can be together, but I also know I won't be able to stop myself from revisiting this moment time and time again.

I finally let sleep take me... I dream that Chance and I are living a different life. A life that allows us to be together like this for always. A single tear runs down my face as I fall into a deeper sleep, one where dreams don't follow me.

Chapter Eighteen
CHANCE

I feel kind of strange today. It's Monday. I'm back at work and everything should be back to normal. The wedding festivities are over and it's definitely back to business as usual here. That would normally make me happy.

When we flew out to Vegas for Sebastian's stag party, I was looking forward to this day; it couldn't come soon enough for me. The thought of getting back into the swing of work was something I could hardly wait for. So, I figured it would be looking forward to today that would get me through Vegas and the wedding.

But now it's here and it's anticlimactic in many ways. Nothing fell apart because I was missing for the best part of a week. No clients fell through the cracks. I don't have a list of angry calls to return, an inbox full of complaints. Instead, I have my normal tasks to do. I know I should be happy about that, but this is the first time I've taken any work time off since I joined the company, so I kind of expected to be missed in some way.

On a rational level, I know it's a good thing. It means my team is dedicated and good at what they do. But on a less rational level, it makes me feel like I'm not really needed here, that I'm not as essential to my area of the business as I thought I was. I know what my father would say to that... he'd tell me that the fact everything went according to plan while I wasn't here is why I'm essential to the business. He would say it means I have a good eye for building a team and that they have my back, even when I'm not there. I try to take comfort in this, but it's still a weird feeling.

But none of that stuff is what's really throwing me off and making me feel strange. I feel that way because a big part of me misses the freedom of not being tied to my desk. Of being able to switch off and actually forget about work for a time. It's not the reaction I was expecting at all, and I don't know quite what to make of it or what to do with it.

And of course, there's Sierra. She's the real reason I'm feeling so off kilter.

As much as I'm trying to convince myself what happened in Vegas will stay there, and by our mutual agreement, what happened at Moorfield Manor was an extension of that, I find my mind wandering back there. I find myself thinking about Sierra in my arms, about her coming hard, shouting my name. And it's not just the sex that lingers. I find myself thinking about her laugh, about the way her eyes would sparkle when she teases me. And I keep thinking about how when we were together, I was lighter. Happier.

But I have to forget about that and move on. We both agreed nothing can happen between us again, and I need to stick to that. I don't want to become one of those lecherous bosses that sees his assistant and pictures her naked. I have to get back into the swing of things here and find the happiness I always got from my work again. Surely, a few fun days can't change my whole outlook on life. I've always been about the job and I've always liked that about myself. I just need a day or two to get back into it.

I nod to myself. That's the only way I can start to feel normal again. I have to forget about the last few days and get back into gear.

I check the time. I have a meeting in ten minutes, but I can't for the life of me remember who it's with. I pick up my desk phone and hold it in my hand for a minute. Sierra will know who the meeting is with. She'll have all of the files and everything I need ready and waiting for me. But I can't bring myself to talk to her. Not yet. Not until I can trust myself to act professional and normal around her.

I call my other assistant, Sandy. I say she's my other assistant, but I rarely work directly with her. If anything, she's Sierra's assistant as Sierra is the one who organizes her workload and gives her all of her tasks based on what Sierra instinctively knows I need doing.

"Good Morning, you've reached..." Sandy says as she takes the call.

"Sandy, it's Chance," I interrupt her.

"Oh, Mr. Hunter. Umm, is everything o-okay?" she stutters. She's clearly shocked that I am calling on her.

"Everything's fine. I have a meeting in ten minutes, but I need to know who it's with and have the relevant paperwork brought to me," I say.

"Okay," she replies. "Sierra is dealing with that, and—"

"And now you're dealing with it," I cut her off again. "Please bring me the information."

I end the call and massage my temples. I feel kind of bad for Sandy, but it's not like I'm asking her to do anything outside of her job description. I know Sierra will have everything ready, Sandy will just need to collect the things I've asked for.

A couple of minutes later, there's a tap on my door.

"Come in," I call.

The door opens and Sandy comes in looking a little flustered. She's holding a stack of papers which she places on my desk in front of me. "Those are the files you asked for. The meeting is with Eric Rutherford and it's about a potential new trade deal. He runs Rutherford's Interiors and you were interested in purchasing wall coverings from him as he's a little cheaper than your current supplier for the same quality products."

I remember now. I remembered when she said his name. Sierra would have known this and not felt the need to waste my time on Eric's back story. I chastise myself, telling myself to give Sandy some slack. It's not her fault she doesn't know how I work. I'm the one who has kept her at arm's length all of the time she's been here, dealing only with Sierra. "Thank you," I say.

She smiles, her cheeks flushing slightly. "Mr. Rutherford is in reception now. Would you like me to show him in?"

"Yes, please."

She nods and practically runs from my office. She returns quickly, Mr. Rutherford in tow, and when she introduces him, her nerves seem to have gone. She's obviously more at home with people than files. She asks if we would like any refreshments.

Eric says no, and so I do as well. Sandy leaves the office and Eric and I begin to talk about what a deal between us would look like.

The meeting goes well and by the end of it, when Eric and I shake hands, we have a deal in place. One that will save the company thousands of dollars, and one that will clearly make Eric a good chunk of money too. These are the deals I relish. The ones where both parties win completely and there will be no hassle anywhere down the line.

"Thanks again Eric. I look forward to us working together. I'll have my assistant put together the paperwork and fax you over a copy."

"It's my pleasure." He smiles. "I'm looking forward to it too." I see him out of the office, purposely avoiding letting my eyes scan the area where Sierra and the other assistants work. I go back into my office quickly and call Sandy. She recognizes the number this time and answers with a, "Yes, Mr. Hunter" instead of the company greeting.

I ask her to get the paperwork ready for Eric and to fax it over. She agrees and I settle back into my chair to start making some calls. As I make my calls, I call on Sandy for several pieces of information, none of which she knows without having to check with Sierra, and then I ask her to schedule a meeting for me for next week.

When I've finished making my calls, I start on my paper inbox, looking over several memos and studying a design idea from one of my designers. I make a few notes on the design and put it in my outbox. I call Sandy to come and collect it and return it.

She appears in my office.

I hand her the design. "This is one of Patrick's. Tell him to take note of the comments I've made and to come to me if he has any questions."

"Okay," she says.

She's heading for the door when I remember I wanted to ask her about Eric's paperwork too. "Sandy?" I say.

She stops and turns back to me, waiting to see what I want.

"Did you send Eric his fax yet? I haven't heard from him and he said he'd confirm with me when he received it."

"Not yet," she says.

I frown. "Why not?" I demand.

"Umm..." She doesn't say anything else, but I can see by her face that she wants to.

"Why not?" I repeat. "Be honest."

She sighs and her face gets a look of resignation on it, a look that says she's going to be honest but that she thinks she'll regret it. "I have a lot of work to get through today Mr. Hunter. I'm not complaining about that. I like to be kept busy. Mr. Rutherford's papers have become a top priority. But..." She stops, looking down at her feet.

"But what?" I demand.

She looks back up at me and she's angry. "But you keep stopping me by asking for clarifications and bookings. The things you're asking me for are all things Sierra deals with and what would be a two second job for her to pull up the information is a twenty minute job for me where I have to redo things Sierra has already done."

I feel a surge of anger inside of myself. It's not about Sandy. Not really. I'm angry at myself because I know she's right. I am wasting everyone's time because of this stupid infatuation I seem to suddenly have with Sierra, which means I feel like I have to avoid her. "I'm pretty sure it's your job to be my assistant Sandy. That means you assist me by completing the tasks I give you. Is that too hard for you?"

"I—no," she says. "But you have to understand that things take time Mr. Hunter, and if you're going to keep coming to me with these things, then you're going to have to accept that I can only do one thing at a time."

"Maybe you would be more efficient if you got on with the tasks instead of standing here arguing with me," I say with a raised eyebrow.

Sandy nods and leaves my office.

I feel instantly guilty. None of this is her fault, but not only am I now piling extra work on her, I'm snapping at her for not being able to do three times as much work in the same amount of time. I make a mental note to apologize to her next time she comes into my office.

I don't have long to dwell on my guilt when there's a knock on my office door. I shout come in.

Patrick appears. "I got your notes. Do you have a minute?" he asks.

I nod and gesture for him to sit down.

He sits down and unrolls his design blueprint. He points to one of my comments. "You say here that this isn't the right place for a feature. I agree, but the client was very specific about wanting this particular feature here. I personally think it will look much better here." He pauses to point out his choice of placing, a placing I would wholeheartedly agree with. "I suggested this to the client and they refused the idea."

"Have you done a virtual walk through video, so the client can see how it will look both our way and theirs?" I ask.

Patrick nods as he pulls out his cell phone and taps the screen a few times. He holds it out to me.

I watch the video walk through of the room designed both ways. I close the video when it's ended. "And?" I say.

He holds his hand out for his phone and makes another few taps. "And this..."

I skim through the email where the client thanks him for his input but sticks to his guns about his original idea. "And you told him this would be more expensive?" I ask.

Patrick nods. "Yes. He said money is no object."

"Okay," I agree. "Well, then in this case, I guess the customer is always right. It won't look as good, but as long as he's seen what it will look like and he's happy with it, there's no reason we can't go ahead with it."

A knock on my door stops me.

"Come in," I shout, expecting Sandy with the files for my next meeting.

Instead, Sierra walks in.

I feel my heart skip a beat and my stomach lurch when I see her. She's back in her sensible knee length pencil skirt and suit jacket, her hair pinned up in a tight little bun. But now all I can see is her hair falling in waves around her shoulders, the flawless white skin of her inner thighs.

"The files for your meeting," she says, holding them up.

All I can hear is her low, husky voice telling me I taste amazing. I take a deep breath and I am accosted by Sierra's scent, a scent that takes me back to coming hard with my face pressed against her neck. I clear my throat and shift in my seat, trying to find a comfortable position as my cock springs to life. "Thank you," I say. "Put them down there please."

"There's a couple of things we need to go over when you're done here," she says.

"I can read, thank you. That won't be necessary," I say.

She raises an eyebrow, but she doesn't argue with me. "As you wish." She leaves the office.

I stare at the closed door for a moment. I can still smell the waft of Sierra's scent that she left behind on the air and it makes me ache for her. I want to get up and follow her out of the office. To lift her up, throw her onto her desk and ravish her body, making her scream for more.

I want to feel her tongue on my body, her hands in my hair. I want to fill her up, feel my cock stretching her pussy, claiming her as mine. I want to lay in bed with her afterwards, holding her in my arms. I want to hear her laugh, to have her tease me and surprise me. I want her to make me feel alive again.

"Umm, Chance?" Patrick says.

I realize I have been staring at the door for too long. I have completely lost my train of thought after seeing Sierra for the first time since Sunday morning when she kissed my cheek, thanked me for the weekend and walked away from me, taking a part of me with her.

"Sorry," I say. "Just thinking about the meeting I've got coming up. Where were we? Ah, yes. If you're confident that the client has seen everything and is happy with the design elements he has chosen, then get this finalized and make a start on it."

"Will do, thanks for your help." He gets to his feet and leaves my office.

I pick up the files Sierra has dropped off, running my fingers softly over the front of them, knowing they're touching the same places her fingers have just touched.

I tell myself to snap out of it. I haven't landed in some slushy romance movie overnight and this is not me. It's like a strange, emotional hangover, that's all. And it will pass. I just have to keep avoiding Sierra until I feel more normal again, and then everything will go back to the way it used to be.

My plan hasn't worked even a little bit. It seems to be the more I try to avoid Sierra, the more she's in my head. It's now Friday and no normal hangover should last this long, but this one only seems to be growing.

I can't get that damned woman out of my head and I'm starting to lose concentration both at work and at home. Every time I push my thoughts of her away and try to focus on the task at hand, she worms her way back into my head, stronger and more insistent than the last time. If this keeps happening, she is going to be completely consuming my thoughts before long.

Last night, I put a pan of spaghetti on. I sat down to check a few emails while it boiled, and somehow, Sierra got into my head again. By the time I remembered what I was supposed to be doing, I had the subject line of one email written, nothing else. And my pan had boiled completely dry.

It's driving me absolutely crazy. I've never ever been with a woman that stays in my head for this long. I don't think I've ever been with a woman who could get into my head at any time of the day or night, regardless of what I'm doing. I know I haven't. I've always made sure I didn't get attached that way. I've never wanted to before, and I believed I had made the decision not to. I always assumed I was strong enough to resist the ridiculous love sick urges other people seemed so quick to succumb to.

Now I know I had it all wrong. I was never strong, never resisting anything. I had just never met anyone I felt strongly enough about to want to think about them when I wasn't with them. It turns out, I'm just as bad as everyone else about separating my emotions and sealing them off when it comes to someone I've grown to care about.

I know I have to find a way though. Sierra and I can't be together, so there's no point in me dwelling on thoughts of her. It's not achieving anything except distracting me and making me miserable.

I've spent the entire week relying on Sandy more and more while avoiding Sierra at all costs. It's not enough though. Knowing she's out there, just on the other side of a wall that no longer seems thick enough, is still enough to make me wonder *what if.* It's still enough to send me on fool's errands to retrieve things I don't need, or to go and talk to someone I don't need to talk to, just to get a glimpse of her. And every time I do get a glimpse of her, I go back to square one, thinking about our time together.

My phone rings and I manage to focus long enough on something other than Sierra to take the call and answer my client's question. I end the call, determined to carry on working while I feel a little more focused. I start to fill in an online order form for some fabric we need for one of our designs. As I fill in the sizes, there's a knock on my office door.

"Yeah," I call.

The door opens and Sierra walks in.

Instantly, any notion I had of being able to concentrate on anything except my thoughts of her vanishes. She gives me an uncertain smile that makes my heart ache. I don't want her to feel like she's done something wrong. She hasn't. This is all my issue, not hers.

I know she must be feeling some of the awkwardness though. I mean she must have noticed that I'm directing all of my communications with my assistants through Sandy now, something that was unheard of before last week. And if she was pissed off about that, she wouldn't have held back from telling me about it. Maybe she's feeling the same inner turmoil as I am. Maybe she's relieved that I've put this wall up and put some distance between us.

She comes forward and stands before my desk, not speaking for a moment.

I see a flicker of something cross her face. Something that looks awfully like the lust I saw in her eyes at Moorfield Mansion. I clear my throat although there's nothing there to be cleared away, a habit I seem to have formed in the last week. Something I do to try and bring my mind into focus when I feel it slipping away again. "What can I do for you Sierra?" I ask.

Other than give you multiple orgasms and make you go wild with desire all night long.

"I just wanted to let you know I've had to reschedule your Monday morning meeting to Wednesday afternoon," she says. "Something came up at the client's end, something he couldn't rearrange." Her tone is business like, her sentences short and clipped like always.

Obviously, she's doing a much better job of forgetting our time together than I am. Or she's a damned good actress. I'm not sure which.

"Okay, thank you." I turn back to my computer, content to leave it at that, needing her out of my office. Her proximity is making it even harder to focus on anything except her and I just need her gone.

"Chance?" she says.

I force myself to keep my face neutral as I look at her. "Yes?" I say, purposely keeping my tone business like, trying to match her composure.

"Nothing," she says, shaking her head and giving me a sad smile. She turns and starts towards the door.

In that moment, I feel it. She's not handling this better than I am; she's just a better actor than I am. I know she's happy for me to be avoiding her because she feels the same way I do. It makes the whole situation that much sadder. If I couldn't get her out of my head, but she was totally over us, then I could accept that. But knowing she wants this too, kills me.

"Sierra, wait," I say.

I'm standing up as she turns around. I need to tell her I get it, that I feel it too, but that we need to just be patient and ride it out until it goes away and we go back to normal again.

Instead, I close the gap between us.

I take her face in my hands and press my lips against hers. Instantly, the taste of her lips engulfs me and my heart is happy again.

My kiss takes her by surprise, and for a moment, she doesn't respond, but then she makes a tiny gasping sound and wraps her arms around my waist, meeting my tongue with hers, her lips moving as frantically as mine as we consume each other's mouths.

My whole body wakes up, raging with the need for this woman. For this moment with her. I know then that I will never be able to go back to the way we were. And Sierra said it herself. She doesn't want to be the woman fucking the boss. She doesn't want this; she doesn't want to be with me. But I can't get her out of my head when I know she's so close and as into me as I am her.

I allow myself another second of her kiss and then I pull away. I take hold of the tops of her arms and gently push her way. "I'm sorry." I turn away and leave my office, not looking back, even though it's the hardest thing I've ever done. It's not as hard as what I know I'm going to have to do next though.

Chapter Twenty

SIERRA

I head into the office on Monday morning with a good feeling inside of me. I'm even humming to myself. Last week was a nightmare. An awful nightmare I felt like I would never wake up from. Chance kept avoiding me like the plague, and I felt horrible about that, but deep down, I was kind of relieved. It's one thing to tell myself I don't want to be that woman at work, the one who sleeps with her boss, but it's quite another to actually believe it.

Chance is a professional through and through, so I know whatever happened between us out of the office wouldn't affect anything in it. If I screwed up, I'd be in trouble, regardless of whether or not I'd sucked his cock the night before. That made it harder to accept that nothing could ever happen between us again.

I found it a little easier because I didn't have to work closely with him all of last week, but I also found it to be a distraction. I found myself watching his office door, desperate for a glimpse of him. And when I got one, it would throw off my concentration completely.

But all of that was something I had anticipated. What I hadn't anticipated was the constant barrage of questions from everyone around me. Sandy wanting to know why she was suddenly Chance's chief point of contact and where the answers to all of his questions would be found. And then the inevitable question; what was going on with us? And the clients and other staff members picked up on our avoidance of each other too, and I found myself constantly fending off questions about whether or not we'd fallen out.

But this week will be better. I know that now, because of what happened on Friday. I came so close to talking to Chance, to asking him when this awkwardness between us would pass. I chickened out of speaking, but it was like he read my mind. He kissed me and for a few moments, everything felt right with the world. It was like he was telling me we'd find a way and everything would be all right.

I've spent the weekend thinking of nothing but Chance and that kiss. Even when Hayley and I went out for ice cream, I was distracted and eventually, I suggested we go and watch a movie, so I could think about him without being distracted from her.

I thought he would call. I thought maybe he would want us to get together over the weekend to talk, or to do something a little more fun than talking, but he hadn't. And that's okay. We can take things slowly. We should take things slowly. At least now, I know he's not avoiding me because he regrets what we did. I debated calling him and a couple of times, I pulled my phone out and got as far as scrolling through my contacts to find his name, but I never got as far as actually calling him.

I think maybe today we'll have some sort of conversation about where we go from here. It's obvious that the attraction I feel to him isn't one sided, and just knowing this has me feeling good. We've been a team for two years in the office. A good team. The A team. And now, we will find a way to be just as good a team outside of it too. It's all about honest communication and we've always had that in work. Now we just have to have it outside of work, and I think we did a good job of that in Vegas and at the wedding. It proves we can make it work if we want to.

I sit down at my desk and fire up my computer. I'm not going to let myself be distracted by this. I'm not going to give anyone a reason to question whether or not I'm off my game, and I'm definitely not going to give Chance a reason to think this is a bad idea because it's affecting my work. I am going to work harder than ever before and show him I am a true professional and that isn't about to change, no matter what changes between us.

I decide to start with my emails. There's always a ton of messages to go through on a Monday morning, like every client, supplier and designer suddenly has a burning question that they just have to send to me at 4am on a Sunday.

I open up my inbox and skim through it, picking out the most important messages to deal with first. My eyes fall to one from HR and I roll my eyes. No doubt another pointless memo about another pointless thing that no one cares about. I debate just deleting it, but I know they keep tabs on who opens their emails and who doesn't, and they will keep resending it to those who don't, until they know everyone has seen the message. It might even require a signature to say I've seen it. I might as well get that out of the way first so I can concentrate on the important messages properly.

I open it and instantly my heart starts to race. This is no random memo. It's addressed directly to me and the line beneath my name makes me feel sick. I read it all twice before I calm down enough to really take it in.

Sierra Lowe,

RE: Transfer to London branch

We would like to offer you our sincere congratulations on your promotion and transfer. While we will be sorry to see you leaving our branch, we know you will do great things in our London office and we wish you all the best in your new role.

We will be faxing the paperwork through to you later today and we just need a signature from you.

If you have any questions or concerns about your transfer, please don't hesitate to reach out,

Kind regards,

Katie Sawyer,

Head of HR

I read it a third time as understanding begins to flood me. I have questions. Plenty of the fucking things. This email reads like I should know what's going on and I have no idea. Except I do. This is Chance's solution to our fling. He wants to send me away. Well, fuck that. I am not going to be tossed aside like a toy he's finished playing with. I can't understand how he thinks it's okay to do this to me. Especially after Friday when he kissed me and let me think there was hope for us.

I get to my feet, my happy mood from only moments ago long gone, replaced with a mixture of anger and sadness that sits heavily on me. I don't quite know what to do with myself; I only know I can't just sit here staring at that offending email any longer. I should go back outside, get some air and calm down, but I don't. I head straight to Chance's office.

I don't care if it is unprofessional to storm in there and go off on him. What is unprofessional would be to transfer someone to the other end of the fucking country because you can't help but feel attracted to them. I mean what sort of playground bullshit is this? So much for us being a team. So much for us being able to communicate effectively with each other.

As I storm down the hallway, part of me is hoping this is all just a terrible misunderstanding. That I'll burst into Chance's office and he won't know what I'm talking about. That he'll fix it all and then we'll laugh about it.

As I push his office door open without knocking, I know that's not the case. His guilt is written all over his face.

"What the hell is going on?" I demand.

"You're the one storming in here with some axe to grind, so why don't you tell me?" Chance says calmly.

His calmness only makes me angrier. How dare he sit there playing like he doesn't know what's going on here? "Don't play games with me, Chance. You know exactly what I'm talking about. A transfer to the London office? Are you insane?"

"Sit down, Sierra," he says gently. "I can see that you're upset."

His gentle tone only serves to anger me further. "I'm not upset, I'm angry," I say, not sitting down. "After everything we talked about, everything we said about keeping ourselves professional, you decide to ship me off to London without even consulting me. That's—that's crazy, Chance. Surely, you see that."

"It's a good move for you. Professionally speaking, it's a promotion that will come with a nice pay rise and a lot of prestige. In two or three years' time, you could be a director. You said you wanted to be successful for Hayley. This is your chance."

"Don't you dare bring Hayley into this!" I snap. "This isn't about her. It's about you. You can't just mess with my life like this."

"It's in your contract that you can be transferred to any branch your services are needed in. You knew that when you took the job."

I am so angry I could burst, but I'm trying my best to rein it in a little. I need him to see that we can move on, that we don't need to be at opposite ends of the country, and ranting and raving is only showing him this is personal.

I finally sit down and I look at Chance until he meets my eyes. The fact I can see regret in his only makes this harder. He isn't sending me away because he hates me; he's sending me away because he likes me and he can't face that.

I take a deep breath and dive in, "I did know that. And at that time, I was willing to travel anywhere I was needed. But things have changed. You can't expect me to pack up and move Hayley to the other end of the world, do you? Away from her grandparents, her school, her friends. She's lost so much, please don't make her lose everything she knows and loves."

"It's out of my hands now," he says.

His voice is calm but I can see the turmoil in his eyes. I have to find a way to make him see he doesn't have to do this. "If you don't want me to be your assistant anymore, I get it. Transfer me to somewhere else in the building. Please?" .

The turmoil fades and his eyes are suddenly stony and cold, like he's flicked some switch inside of himself and turned his emotions off.

I wish I could do the same, but I can't.

"I'm sorry. This isn't open for discussion. You will spend the rest of the week here getting your affairs in order and you'll be expected in London in two weeks' time."

"And that's your final word on the subject?" I ask.

He nods his head firmly "It is. Now if you'll excuse me, I have a call to make," he says.

I sit for another second, forcing myself to swallow past the lump in my throat. "Then I might as well give you my final word on the subject," I say, pleased my voice comes out sounding level. "I quit. Effective immediately. I trust that you won't try to stop me or sever my bonus?"

"If that's what you want, then no, I won't do either of those things. Your final paycheck will be forwarded to you and I'll see that HR provides you with a glowing reference. Goodbye Sierra."

His words are the final blow. They sting like he's cut me. I really thought he would come to his senses and fight for me, if not as anything personal, then at least as a valued member of staff. I nod curtly and stand up. I leave the office and go to my desk long enough to grab my handbag from the floor. I turn and walk away. I can hear Sandy calling after me, but I don't turn around. I don't want her to see the tears shining in my eyes.

How the hell did it come to this? Even as I was sleeping with Chance, I knew it was a mistake. I knew we could never be more than just a fling. I knew I was risking losing my heart to him, but I didn't know I was risking losing everything. My career, the job I've worked so hard for. It's all gone. I think Chance will keep his word and make sure I get a glowing reference, but that's hardly much comfort. I deserve a glowing reference because I'm damned good at what I do. I don't deserve this though. To be shipped off, thrown away like trash, just so Chance doesn't have to face his mistake every day.

I can't believe I thought that there was hope for us. I had also believed Chance felt the same way I did and that somehow, someway, we had a shot of making things work out between us. I was naïve. So naïve. And I have no one to blame for this but myself. I should have been strong and just walked away. Now I have no choice on either score.

Chapter Twenty-One

CHANCE

It's been over two weeks since Sierra left the company. I told Matt and Sebastian she left due to personal reasons and they seemed to accept my explanation. I mean it's not really a lie. I tried to send her to another branch and she refused to go. That's a personal circumstance right? It's most certainly a circumstance neither of my brothers need to know about, and they have no reason to dig any deeper. If one of them told me one of their assistants had left the company, I wouldn't feel the need to involve myself in it and they have the same attitude to my side of things.

I honestly thought I would feel better by now. That having her gone would stop me thinking about her. It hasn't. Not even close. She's on my mind twenty-four hours a day, seven days a week, and I'm starting to think that won't ever change, that she's just moved into my head and is setting up camp there.

And now, it's not just thinking about how amazing she is. It's thinking about how massively I screwed up. I wish I could have just talked to her, to have explained to her how I felt and told her I just needed some time to go back to normal with her. She might have been hurt or angry, but not as hurt or angry as she is now. I think she would have understood and if nothing else, she would have been happy that I was at least honest with her.

At least that way, my thoughts of her wouldn't have been all regrets. I've caused all of this shit and I've achieved nothing. I'm still consumed by Sierra. I still can't concentrate on work. And for what?

Nothing, that's what.

A knock on my office door pulls me out of my thoughts, but not for long, because my instant reaction to the knocking is that I don't know who will be at my door, but I know it won't be Sierra. And it should be Sierra. She's the only person I want to see right now.

"Come in," I shout, trying to hide my resentment at being disturbed.

Sandy sticks her head around the door. "I'm just reminding you about your meeting at four."

I stare at her blankly for a moment, wishing she was Sierra.

"You told me to remind you," she says, looking a little bit lost, like she's not sure what to do with my blank stare.

I blink and force myself to focus on Sandy and act like a normal person for a moment. "Yes, thank you. Is everything ready?"

She nods her head. "Yes. Everything's in place in the conference room like you asked."

"Thank you," I say again.

. . .

*S*he nods and closes the door softly behind her as she retreats.

The day Sierra left, I called her into my office and promoted her to my chief assistant. I told her I had been prepping her to take over the role and that's why I had been relying on her more heavily the previous week. I don't know whether or not she believed me, but if she didn't, she pretended to and gratefully accepted the promotion.

My personal phone vibrates in my pocket. I pull it out and my heart lurches when I see Sierra's name on the screen. She's sent me a text message. Is this her reaching out to say she forgives me? Maybe even that she wants to see me? Because if it is, then what's stopping me now? It's not like we work together anymore. We could actually be together now, without it being unprofessional.

My hopes are dashed when I open the text message. It's straight to the point. Sierra's messages have always been straight to the point, but this time, I was hoping for more.

Just to inform you our annulment has been granted. The courts will send out the paperwork over the next few days.

I should feel relieved. At least there won't be an awkward and expensive divorce proceeding to go through this way, but I'm not relieved. I'm sad. It's like the final goodbye. Like Sierra is officially no longer part of my life in any way. At least, if this had failed, then I would have gotten to see her again. Now there is nothing to tie us together anymore.

I send her a quick reply, as courteous and to the point as her message was.

Thank you for sorting everything and for letting me know.

The Chance and Sierra who spent a brief but fantastic time together would have been laughing and cracking jokes about this, but those people are gone, and we're left with the business like coldness we've always had. And after this short exchange, there won't even be that.

I am so tempted to send her another message, asking her to have a drink with me, but I already know what she'd say. I start to put my phone away, and then I decide against it. I can't ask Sierra to go for a drink with me – that would be stupid and a guaranteed way to get rejected - but I sure as hell need a drink anyway. So instead, I text Nathan, a good friend of mine, asking him if he's free for drinks tonight.

He responds quickly saying he can't stay out too late as he has a big meeting in the morning, but that he'd love to grab a quick one after work.

We make the arrangements and I feel a little better. It's got to be better to go out for a few hours than just sit at home staring at the walls thinking of, well... her.

The rest of the working day drags like mad, something I've never experienced before. I've always been happiest in the office. I'd lost count of the times in the past when I checked my watch to discover it's after midnight and I'm still happily working away. Now, I'm struggling to get through until five o'clock with my sanity in some sort of tact.

Five o'clock finally rolls around and I leave the office to barely concealed looks of shock from Sandy and the rest of the team. I go outside and head for the bar I'm meeting Nathan at, leaving my car at the office.

I step into the bar. It's busy but not so busy it's uncomfortable. Nathan waves at me from a table as I make my way towards the bar. I give him a thumbs up and get myself a drink and then I go to join him.

"So what's up?" he asks as I sit down.

"Does something have to be up for us to have a drink?" I ask.

"No," he says with a grin. "But something has to be up for us to have a drink before ten as you won't leave the office any earlier than that."

God, was I really this boring before Vegas? I don't know, but I still miss those days. The days when my mind was filled with work orders and paint samples, instead of misery and regret. Things were easier then. Logical.

"I just wanted a drink." I shrug to Nathan.

"Who is she?" he asks.

"Huh?" I ask, surprised.

"Only a woman causes a guy to get that look on his face." Nathan laughs.

I sigh. He's seen clean through me and instead of taking my mind off Sierra, he has it straight back on her. I decide to just be honest with him. Maybe he can tell me how the hell to move on and not feel like this anymore. "She was my assistant. We made a mistake and slept together. She's left the company now, and I don't know what to do. I just can't get her out of my mind."

"So call her," Nathan says, like it's that easy.

"It's not that simple," I tell him.

I explain everything to him. Everything except our accidental wedding.

When I've finished talking he nods and smiles. "Well, you definitely fucked that one up in style didn't you?" he says.

I nod my head and grimace. "Oh, yeah."

"Look I don't mean to be an insensitive dick, but you worked with this woman for two years and never felt even the tiniest bit of attraction to her. Have you considered the fact that she could just be a good lay and that's why you keep thinking of her?"

I have considered it. I've tried my best to make myself believe it too.

"There's a good way to find out," Nathan adds when I don't reply.

"I can't call her," I say.

"I wasn't suggesting you should. I was suggesting you should move on. Sleep with someone else. You'll soon forget her and realize it was just a fling."

"Maybe that's exactly what I need to do," I say.

"I'm telling you, it's the way forward." He laughs.

The topic of conversation moves on and as Nathan catches me up with what's going on with his business, for a few hours, I actually manage to forget about Sierra.

He downs his drink. "Well, I'd better get going. It was good to catch up with you."

"Yeah, good to catch up with you too. I think I'll have one more and then I'll probably head home too."

He stands up and claps me on the shoulder. "Yeah, you remember what I said earlier? About moving on?"

I nod.

"Good, because blondie there at the bar has been giving you the eye for the last hour. Go on over and say hello." He disappears with a final call of see you later.

I fix my attention on the table for a moment, but I can't resist peeking up after a few minutes. He's right about the blonde girl at the bar. She's sitting on a bar stool, facing into the room and every few seconds, her eyes flicker towards me.

She looks about the same age as me, pretty and slim. She's no Sierra, but she's attractive and I guess it can't hurt to buy her a drink and talk to her for a bit. And if one thing leads to another, maybe Nathan will be right and it will make me see Sierra was just a flight of fancy.

I finish the last bit of my drink and head towards the bar, purposely making a bee line for the part of the bar where the woman is sitting. I reach the bar. The bartender is busy serving someone else. I decide if I don't speak to the woman now, I'm probably going to lose my nerve. "Hi," I say to her. "Are you waiting for someone?"

She shakes her head. "No. I was meant to be meeting a friend here after work, but there was some sort of emergency and she had to stay over and work. I wanted a drink, so I thought why not."

"Why not indeed." I smile. "I'm Chance. Mind if I join you?"

"Sure." She smiles.

I sit down on the bar stool next to her.

She swivels around so she's facing me. "I'm Tiffany."

The bartender moves to me and I ask for a rum and coke.

"Would you like a drink Tiffany?" I ask.

"Malibu and coke please," she says.

I get her the drink and smile at her as she thanks me, suddenly completely lost for words. "So do you come here a lot?" I mentally kick myself for the clichéd question. I mean God, I might as well have just walked over here and told her I was desperate.

"Not much. You?" she says.

I shrug. "No. Not really."

We lapse into a silence, an awkward silence that's stretching out for far too long. I try my best to think of something interesting to say, but I fail miserably and resort instead to my favorite subject; work. "What do you do for a living?" I ask.

"I'm an escort," she says.

"An escort?" I reply, shocked.

She bursts into laughter. "I'm joking. I work in retail. I'm a buyer for a boutique fashion brand."

I can't help but laugh. "You had me there," I say, relaxing a little. "Do you enjoy your job?"

"Yes." She nods. "I basically get paid to shop. I think it's most women's dream job."

I'm not so sure about that. Sierra would hate it. I shake my head. Now isn't the time to let Sierra back into my thoughts.

"What do you do?" Tiffany asks.

"I work as an interior designer within my family's business," I say.

"Oh," she replies, clearly surprised. She laughs. "Now, you're playing me right? Getting your own back."

"No why?" I ask, surprised by her reaction.

She looks me up and down and shakes her head. "I just figured someone who was a designer would be dressed more casually. Maybe even sporting a paint splatter or two." She laughs.

"Common misconception." I smile. "On a bad day, you might catch me with ink splats from my designs, but I don't actually get involved in the decorating, I just design the place."

"Do you ever find that you have this vision in your mind and the decorators are just way off when they've finished?" she asks.

"Not so much now. I work with a trusted team who get me and understand my visions for a space, but in the past, yes, regularly. You sound like you're speaking from experience. Have you been in this field?"

She shakes her head. "No, but part of my job is outlining how I want the window and in store displays to look, and you have no idea how many times I've just given up and done it myself to get it to look right."

"Oh, I can well imagine," I agree.

We share a few stories of our disasters and I find myself relaxing again and soon, my laughter is genuine. Tiffany is a nice girl and maybe Nathan was right, because as we move onto our next drink, I find myself warming to her.

We're still sitting at the bar laughing and chatting when the bartender calls last orders. I ask Tiffany if she'd like another one, but she declines saying she had better call a cab. I nod and she slips off her stool and goes to make the call. She comes back for her handbag and I stand up and walk her outside.

I am suddenly awkward again. I like Tiffany, but I don't find her attractive in the way I find Sierra attractive. Is it really fair to Tiffany to take this any further knowing I'd only be using her to try to forget Sierra? I already know the answer to that question, but maybe it'll be okay if I make it clear this is a one night thing and she might be up for that. Although that didn't exactly work with Sierra did it?

"What's wrong?" Tiffany asks.

I shake my head and smile. "Nothing."

"Yes, there is. You've gone all weird on me. Is it because you're nervous? Don't worry, I'm a sure thing." She laughs.

That does it. I don't want a sure thing with Tiffany. I want an unpredictable, messy thing with Sierra. "I'm sorry, you're a nice girl and everything, and I've enjoyed your company tonight, but anything else would be a mistake."

"You have a girlfriend?" she says, a little dejected.

"No. I'm no cheat. I just—there's this girl I'm into that isn't into me and I thought I was ready to move on, but I'm not. I'm sorry."

She shakes her head. "You don't need to say you're sorry. These things happen. And I appreciate your honesty. For what it's worth, I think she's an idiot if she's not into you." She smiles.

I return her smile. I wish it was that simple. It was at one time. Sierra was into me. And then I fucked everything up.

"You don't have to wait here you know," she says when I don't reply.

"Of course, I do. I might not be ready for being with someone else, but that doesn't make me a total jerk. I'll still make sure you get into your cab safely."

She laughs softly. "Then you're already a better guy than most of the ones I date."

"Don't settle for anything less than what you deserve," I say.

"I could say the same thing to you," she replies.

I frown.

She laughs. "Look, I don't know what went on with you and this girl, but if you're this hung up on her, call her and tell her how you feel. She might not want to date you, but at least you'll know you gave it your best shot. On the other hand, she might be feeling exactly the same and thinking you're not into her. What have you got to lose?"

"My pride," I admit.

"Ah, there's no place for that in a relationship. Call her," Tiffany says.

I am really tempted to take her advice. I took Nathan's advice about moving on and that turned out to be shit. Maybe Tiffany's advice will work out better. But I know I can't call her now. Not when I'm tipsy. I vow to myself I'll call her first thing in the morning.

Tiffany's cab pulls up.

"Can I drop you anywhere?" she asks.

"No, I'm going to walk home. I need a bit of air. But thanks for tonight and for the advice. I'm going to call her in the morning."

"Good for you." Tiffany gets into her cab. "Good night and good luck."

"Good night," I reply as I watch her cab pulling away, then I turn and set off towards home. I need to try with Sierra. God, I really, really hope I'm not too late.

It's funny, because when Tiffany and I talked before she got into her cab, I felt a tiny flicker of hope inside of me that this would all work out for the best. Now as I walk the quiet streets alone with my thoughts, I feel more dejected and hopeless than I had since the morning Sierra quit her job.

Chapter Twenty-Two

CHANCE

I woke up early this morning, long before the sun came up. I was instantly filled with thoughts of Sierra. I still want to call her. The idea hasn't faded away and although, I'm terrified of what her reaction will be, Tiffany's words hang in my head. The two options. She either feels the same way as I do and she is just waiting for this call, or she doesn't and at least this way, I'll know for sure.

I thought about the phone call the whole time I showered and dressed then all the way through my first cup of coffee. I want to call her right now, but it's still so early and I don't want to wake her to have this conversation and start off by pissing her off before I've even opened my mouth. I decide to have breakfast and then call her.

I go to the fridge and pull out a small tub of yogurt. I'm too nervous to eat much more and after a couple of spoons of it, I realize I'm too nervous to even eat that. I throw the remaining yogurt away and check the time. It's almost seven and if Sierra has found another job, she'll definitely be up now. She probably will be anyway, so she can make sure

Hayley gets all sorted for school on time. I know now, I'm only procrastinating because I am afraid to make the call, so I stand up purposefully and grab my phone.

What's the worst thing that could happen? Well, she could tell me to fuck off and rip my heart out. But is that really any worse than this limbo of not knowing if there could be a chance for us? I really don't think it is. I think right now, the worst thing that could happen is that I lose my nerve and don't make this call.

I scroll through my contacts and my heart skips a beat at the sight of Sierra's name. I press call quickly before I can change my mind and I begin to pace the room as I listen to the phone ringing.

I am about to give up; she clearly has seen my name on her screen and decided against taking the call. I guess that tells me everything I need to know without the indignity of me having to beg her to hear me out. I start to move the phone from my ear when her voice is in my head, and this time, it's there for real.

"Hello," she says, somewhat breathlessly.

"Is this a bad time?" I ask.

"No," she says. "I was just upstairs and I forgot my phone was downstairs until I heard it ringing. What can I do for you?"

She started out friendly, a conversational tone that gives me hope this mess between us can be salvaged. As she asks what she can do for me, her voice hardens and I know it won't be easy to convince her to give me a chance. But I don't care if it's hard, as long as it's possible.

"You can forgive me for being a massive asshole," I say.

That gets a soft laugh and I imagine I can feel her warm breath on my ear.

"Is that an apology?" she asks.

"No, but this is. Sierra, I'm so sorry. I let my feelings get in the way of my professionalism, something I promised myself I wouldn't do. And you paid the price. And I really am sorry."

"Thank you," she says, but she doesn't say anything else.

I hurry on in case she tries to end the call. I just have to get this all out and make her understand while I have her on the line, "The thing is, I miss you. Not just in the office but everywhere. I've never stopped thinking about you since you left and it's driving me crazy. I have to know if there is any chance whatsoever of us maybe trying to go on a date or something," I blabber. "I have tried to stop myself from thinking about you. To move on. I talked to a friend and he said I should try dating someone else to get you out of my mind, and I had my chance last night. I was with a woman and ..."

"You were with a woman," she interrupts.

"Yes. But not like that. I just got talking to her in a bar, and I realized she wasn't you Sierra."

"And I'm supposed to be what? Pleased that you compared me to some other woman and I won? Wow Chance, I didn't think you were that sort of guy," she says.

"No, Sierra, you don't understand," I reply.

"Actually, I do understand," she snaps. "I understand perfectly well. You thought you could forget about me by sleeping with someone else and it didn't work, so now you are calling me."

"I didn't sleep with her," I protest feebly.

"Maybe not, but it still took a night with someone else for you to even think about apologizing, let alone anything else," she says. "Listen, do me a favor and just leave me alone alright? Don't call me again."

Dammit. I've really lost her now. I blabbered everything out and it came out all wrong and now she's even more angry with me than she was in the first place. She sounded like she was actually on the verge of forgiving me too, until I started in about last night. "Wait, please don't hang up. Let me explain," I plead.

"I don't need an explanation. We're not together. You can do what you want with whoever you want to do it with. And if it makes you feel any better, I accept your apology. I have come to realize how much more there is to life than just working all day every day. Hayley and I have spent so much time together and we're getting closer every day. And I've even given some thought to getting out, maybe to another city like you wanted me to. In fact, I'm making plans to do just that. So you're forgiven."

"I—you're leaving town?" I ask, deflated.

"Yes. Goodbye, Chance," she says and ends the call.

Fuck! That was even worse than I imagined it would be. I finally decided it was time to fight for Sierra, and now I'm too late. She's leaving. I almost throw my phone across the room, but I think better of it. If she changes her mind and calls me back, I don't want to miss that call. I know she won't though. I could hear the steel in her voice when she told me to leave her alone and not call her again.

I'm not going to do that. I won't. I... I can't. I have to make her see I know I was an asshole but I've changed and that I will never ever hurt her again. I have to get her to talk to me, and once I've explained everything, I think she'll understand. But how do I get her to talk to me?

I sit down on the couch and rub my hands over my face. Dating and romance isn't my area. Obviously. If it was, I wouldn't have made such a spectacular mess of this.

I think about my friends and who would have any idea how to fix this. My thoughts keep going back to one person... Matt. When he first met Callie, he made a terrible job of it all and a big misunderstanding almost kept them apart. But he didn't give up on her. He fought for her and proved himself to her. And if I want to do the same thing for Sierra, which I do more than anything, then I'm going to have to swallow my pride and ask Matt for his help. It'll mean telling him everything, but I'm willing to do that if it gives me even a half a chance of getting Sierra back.

I pull my phone out again, and call Matt.

He answers quickly, "Hey bro, what's up?"

"Can you come over before work?" I ask. "I need to talk to you about something."

"Is everything all right?" he asks.

"Not really..." I sigh. "But I think it can be. If you're willing to help me."

"Sure. I'll be right over," Matt says.

I end the call and go back to pacing the living room while I wait for Matt to show up.

Matt shows up after what feels like forever but in reality is probably no longer than half an hour.

By the time he arrives, I've managed to calm myself down, work myself back up into a frenzy then calm down again. I'm jittery, nervous, but I don't feel like a complete wreck now... I'm ready to take action.

"What's up?" Matt asks as he comes in and sits down.

"You're not going to believe this, but just hear me out okay?" I ask.

Matt nods. He looks a little nervous himself now, like he's not quite sure what bombshell I'm going to drop on him. He will be more than shocked when he hears this is about a woman. I have no doubt that at the moment, he's most likely thinking it's about work.

"Something did happen in Vegas between Sierra and me," I say.

I wait for Matt's mouth to drop open, for him to exclaim in surprise but he just nods. I narrow my eyes at him.

He lets out a laugh. "Come on," he says. "Like I told you at the time, it started out as a joke but when I spoke to you outside of the restaurant, it was clear to me that something had happened. So what went down?"

"Basically, we woke up in bed together that morning with no recollection of the night before. We talked and started to piece together bits of what happened, and somewhere along the way, I got to know Sierra as a person and not just as my assistant. We ended up together again and we both agreed it would stay in Vegas."

"But?" Matt prompts me.

"But it happened again at Sebastian's wedding. We agreed that would definitely be the end of it. We had one glorious night to share, and then we'd be back to professional."

"Right," Matt says thoughtfully. "But obviously that didn't work out did it?"

"What makes you say that?" I ask.

"The fact you called me to tell me this," Matt says. "So you two got back home, realized you had something special and Sierra stopped working for you?"

"I wish it was that simple," I say shaking my head.

I sit down opposite Matt and run my hands over my face. I look up and meet his eye for a moment and then I look away. This is hard enough to talk about without having to watch Matt's face as I explain just how spectacularly I fucked up.

"I thought I would go back to work after the wedding and just forget about what had happened. But I found myself thinking of Sierra constantly, and it was getting to the point where I was losing focus. I tried my best to avoid her, but of course that just made my longing for her worse. She came into my office one day and I just couldn't help myself any longer. I grabbed her and kissed her, and that's when I knew something had to give. I was acting unprofessional and I hated it. I arranged for Sierra to be transferred to our London branch, and—"

"You did what?" Matt exclaims.

"I arranged for her to be transferred to our London branch. It wasn't a made up spot, there was a position open that would have suited her perfectly and it was a promotion and came with a nice pay rise."

"But if she wanted to go to London, she might have told you that," Matt says.

"Yeah. Exactly. To say I screwed up on that one would be the understatement of the century. She was pissed off to say the least, and knowing I had upset her bothered me way more than it should. So I switched off, became detached. I told her it wasn't open for discussion and she quit."

"Shit," Matt says. "That explains her sudden departure then. Mind you, I wouldn't have guessed her personal reason was you being a dick. Although, I maybe should have."

"Yeah yeah, you're not telling me anything I don't already know here. I know I was a dick, I just don't know how to fix it," I say.

"You want her to come back?" Matt asks.

"No. Not unless she wants to. That isn't what this is about. I-I have feelings for her Matt. Even now, I can't stop thinking about her. I really want to get her to forgive me and give us a chance, but the more I try to fix things, the worse I seem to make them. And I don't know what to do. She's talking about leaving, and then I'll never see her again. I have to find a way to stop her from going, but I don't know how to do that. That's why I need your help. I mean you fucked up pretty bad with Callie in the beginning but she forgave you. How did you make her come around?"

"Hold on. Are you saying you're in love with Sierra?" Matt asks.

I pause for a second. Is that what I'm saying? I don't know if it is really what I wanted to say, but I do know it's exactly what I feel. I nod my head and finally meet his eyes. Instead of the amusement I expect to see there, I see his mind working overtime.

"Okay. So if you want to get her to stay, then you have to put yourself out there and give her a reason to stay. Tell her how you feel. That's how I got Callie to come around. I was honest with her about my feelings."

"Yeah, I've already tried that and I made it worse," I say.

"What did you say that could be worse than trying to send her to another country?" Matt asks.

"I told her how I feel about her," I say.

Matt laughs softly. "No... this is you. Your idea of telling her how you feel probably ended up in you insulting her or something."

I sigh. He's not exactly wrong about that one. "I went for a drink with Nathan last night. I told him a bit about this, and he convinced me I wasn't really into Sierra, that she was just a good lay and that's what I was fixating on. He told me to get laid and said I would feel different."

"Oh, you didn't?" Matt exclaims.

"No. Not exactly. I got to talking to a girl in the bar and she was nice, attractive too and I enjoyed her company. But when it came down to it, all it did was make me see that it was about a lot more than just sex with Sierra. I put the girl in a cab and came home alone. It was this morning when the real problem started. I knew I had to win Sierra back, so I called her. I apologized for being a douchebag, and I think she was starting to come around, I really do. So I launched into this speech about how I didn't want anyone else but her, and how last night proved that."

"You told Sierra you had to be with someone else to realize you had feelings for her?" Matt asks, incredulous.

His reaction is pretty much the same as Sierra's, except his hurts a whole lot less than hers did.

"Pretty much, yeah. She told me to leave her alone and never call her again. So what do I do Matt? Because I'm not ready to let her go. I'm not even close to being ready for that."

"Wait until I tell Callie about this. She'll realize that me lying about who I really was is nothing compared to sleeping with someone else to see if you like a person!" Matt laughs.

"I didn't sleep with her!" I insist.

"Oh I know, but in my version of the story, you will have." He grins.

"Look I'm glad you find this amusing. Don't make me regret telling you this Matt. Tell me what I need to say to get her back. If you even think it's possible."

"It's possible," Matt says with a certainty I wish I felt.

"How can you be so sure?" I ask.

"Because of her reaction. If she didn't care about you at all, she wouldn't have been upset about you being with someone else. She does know you weren't with her, with her right?"

I nod my head.

"Good. Then this is fixable. But you're not going to like my answer."

"Just tell me," I say. "I'm ready to try anything."

"Good, because actions speak louder than words. Sierra isn't going to believe you if you just keep bombarding her with words. Especially, because you're so useless at choosing the right ones," he states flatly.

I glare at him and he shrugs. We both know he's right. I roll my eyes and gesture for him to go on. I'm getting off lightly really. I expected him to relish this moment and really rub it in, but he's not.

"You need to get out of your own head and stop being so worried about showing her how you feel," he says.

"You're talking in riddles, Matt. Tell me what you mean."

"I mean you need to make a grand romantic gesture and show Sierra how much she means to you," he says.

I had an awful feeling he was going to say this and I'm already shaking my head before he's even finished talking. "I can't do that. Big romance isn't my style."

"So let her go then," Matt says.

"I can't do that either."

"Well, you need to do one or the other," he says.

I sigh. Why can't this be simple? Other people make it look simple. But other people probably haven't spent so many years closed off to even the idea of love. "Ok. Let's say I agree to do something big. What would it be?"

"I have no idea." Matt shrugs.

"Oh thanks, that's really useful," I say. "Don't spend too long thinking about it or anything."

Matt laughs softly. "It's not that I'm not thinking about it. It's that I genuinely don't know. I know what I would do for Callie, but I don't know Sierra that well. You need to figure out what will work on her. What will show her that you've thought about her and that you know her inside and out. Or at the very least show her that you're willing to put yourself out there and try."

I nod my head slowly as I digest the idea. It's not me, but I said I was willing to do whatever it took to get Sierra back, and I meant it. So if I have to put myself out there and risk showing myself up, then that's what I'll do. My mind is whirling with ideas and one keeps coming back time and time again. I keep pushing it away, worried that it's too big, or that I'll do it and she'll reject me, but I know I have to try.

I stand up and smile. "I know what I'm going to do. Holy shit, I actually know what I'm going to do," I say, starting to laugh.

I really think this might work. And if it doesn't, then at least I won't have any regrets. I'll know I did everything I could to try to prove to Sierra that I can change, that I can be the man she deserves.

I head for the door and look back over my shoulder. "Thanks bro. Can you see yourself out? I have some stuff I need to take care of."

Matt nods, laughing. "Go get her," he shouts after me.

Oh, I intend to. I send a quick text to Sandy telling her to cancel my day and then I head to my car and start putting my plan into action.

Chapter Twenty-Three

CHANCE

I drive along in the direction of Sierra's house. It feels strange because I'm not in my car. I'm driving a huge truck. I never pictured myself driving a truck, but then again, I never pictured myself falling in love and making a cheesy grand romantic gesture for the woman I love.

And here's the thing... I get it now.

Now I know what it feels like to love someone and to allow myself to admit that, the romantic gesture doesn't feel cheesy anymore. It feels right.

I just hope Sierra sees it that way. I'm so nervous my hands keep slipping off the steering wheel where my palms are sweating. My throat is bone dry and each breath hurts a little but I don't care. My heart is racing.

I pull up outside of her house and jump down from the truck cab. Adrenaline is flooding through my body, leaving a coppery taste in my mouth and making my legs feel like jelly. I tell myself to get a grip as I open the back doors to the truck. I grin at the sight inside. The whole truck is filled with red roses; thousands of them.

Two men sit amongst them all, ready to start taking the flowers in.

"Ready?" I ask them.

They nod and scramble out of the truck.

"Good luck," one of them says, clapping me on the shoulder.

"Thanks," I say.

I go back to the cab but I don't get back in it. Instead, I lay on the horn for a few seconds, blasting out noise. I jump back from sight, watching round the edge of the truck as the men arrive at Sierra's door with the first of the flowers.

She comes to the door, looking puzzled when she sees the truck.

"Delivery for Sierra Lowe," one of the men says.

"That's me," Sierra replies.

"Then I suggest you move aside because there's more where these came from." The man laughs.

Sierra frowns in confusion, but she does as he says and the men troop into the house. They come back to the truck and load up again. Sierra's eyes are rounding as they move in and out of the truck, filling her whole house with flowers.

After a few minutes, Sierra snaps out of the shock and stops one of the men. "Wait," she says. "What's this all about? Who are these from?"

This is my moment. I move back into the cab of the truck and grab the big bunch of roses from the passenger seat and then I smile to myself as I hit play on the CD player. Marvin Gaye's Let's Get It On blasts from the cab.

This attracts Sierra's attention.

It's not a song I would like to think of as our song, but I can't hear it without thinking of our cab ride in Vegas and I hope it has the same effect on her. I think maybe it does, because as I step from behind the truck and move into her line of sight, I see her smile wistfully for a moment before she sets her face.

That momentary smile tells me I still have a chance here.

I approach her, holding out the bunch of flowers.

She smiles again, as she takes them and then she looks at me questioningly. "I didn't pick you as a romantic gesture kind of guy," she says softly.

"That's because I'm not. But I'm willing to try to change that if you'll just hear me out."

She sighs.

For a moment, I think she's going to tell me no, but then she gives me a barely perceptible nod. I might have imagined it, but I'm not waiting to find out.

"Sierra, I've handled this whole thing horribly. Since the moment you arrived in Vegas, I've messed up time and time again, each time a little bit more spectacular than the last. It's taken me this long to work out why. It's because... it's because I'm in love with you, and honestly, I don't quite know what to do with that or how to act. But I want to learn. I want to learn with you. Will you give me a chance to do that? Will you go on a date with me tonight?"

Sierra opens her mouth to reply when a soft voice comes from behind her and she stops.

"Aunt Sierra? What's going on?" the voice asks.

I look down and see a little girl dressed in jeans and a pink unicorn t-shirt. She has Sierra's sparkling eyes and she has long brown hair that she pushes behind her ears. She stands behind Sierra's legs and peers out at me.

I smile at her and she smiles back, a shy smile, but a smile all the same.

Sierra turns and crouches down at the girl's level. "Hayley, this is Chance. He sent us all of these flowers. Isn't that nice of him?"

Hayley nods and then she looks at me again, and this time, her smile is wider, the innocent, happy smile of a child.

"I thought the two most beautiful girls I know deserved some flowers that are almost as beautiful as they are," I say.

Hayley giggles.

Sierra straightens back up. "Go on inside honey, I'll be in soon," she says.

Hayley gives me a little wave and she skips off back into the house.

"You were saying?" Sierra says.

"I'm so sorry, Sierra. I'm sorry for everything. But most of all, I'm sorry that I didn't tell you how I felt about you sooner."

"No. That's not what you were saying," she says.

I can see the sparkle in her eyes, the one she gets when she's teasing me.

"You were asking me on a date," she prompts me.

"Yeah, indeed I was," I reply. "I would love to have a date with you and talk to you and see if there's any chance for us. Can I pick you up tonight at eight or is that too short notice for Hayley?"

"Tonight at eight is perfect," she smiles. "Where will we be going?"

"It's a surprise," I say.

"You mean you have no idea because you weren't convinced I'd say yes?" she says with a laugh.

"No," I reply. "Well, yes and no. I wasn't convinced you'd say yes, because I know myself and I was sure I'd find a way to fuck this up further. But I already know exactly what we'll be doing tonight, don't worry about that."

"Okay." Sierra laughs. "I believe you. These flowers have set the bar pretty high though."

"Yeah, I really should have started smaller." I laugh.

Chapter Twenty-Four

SIERRA

When I saw Chance appear around the side of the truck's cab this afternoon and worked out that all of the flowers were from him, I felt myself melting inside. I really wanted to stay angry with him after everything he had done to me, but I just couldn't. And when he spoke to me, told me he wanted us to try to make things work, I knew if I said no, I would only be spitting on myself. I knew I owed it to both of us to at least give him a chance.

When he admitted to being in love with me, my heart almost burst with joy and I knew then I would be going on this date with him. I can forgive the mess he's made of all of this. I mean it's not like I don't know him. I knew this wouldn't be easy for him, but he's definitely trying and the fact he's making such a big effort to make this all up to me tells me he's worth trying.

I'm not quite ready to swoon into his arms just yet though. He has to show me he's for real this time. That he's not going to run at the first sign of things not fitting into a neat little box he can file away somewhere in his head.

I smile at my reflection in the mirror. I never dared to dream I would ever meet someone like Chance. But now I have, staying neutral and not confessing that I feel the same way about him is going to be pretty much impossible to do. The way I feel about him is written all over my face. It's in my slightly flushed cheeks, my carefree smile. It's even in my posture. My shoulders have lost their stiffness. I feel different. Lighter somehow.

A little knock sounds on my bedroom door and I turn to the already half open door. Hayley comes in and smiles when she sees my short black dress and high black patent leather heels. "You look so pretty Auntie Sierra."

"Thank you," I say.

She sits down on my bed and looks at me for a second. "And you're going out with flower man?" she asks.

"His name is Chance." I laugh. "But yes."

"You should marry him," she states, like that's the obvious solution to all of our problems.

Maybe it is. I mean it wouldn't be the first time. Our first date was technically our own wedding. "I think it's a bit soon to be thinking about that."

"Why? You love him," she says.

God, how is she so clued in already? "Let's just see how tonight goes for now," I say.

She smiles knowingly. "Whatever," she says. "He's here by the way."

My heart skips a beat as I imagine him downstairs waiting for me.

"Come on," she urges.

I take one last glance into the mirror and then I follow Hayley down the stairs as she excitedly skips ahead of me.

"Penny said he's handsome," she whispers in a voice loud enough for the whole street to have heard her.

Penny is my neighbor's sixteen year old daughter who is watching Hayley for me tonight. And she must be mortified now because her and Chance must have heard Hayley's announcement.

"And what do you think?" I ask.

"I agree," she states.

I rub the top of her head as we reach the bottom of the stairs.

She leads the way into the lounge and my heart skips another beat as Chance stands up as I enter. He's wearing jeans and a black shirt and he looks so good. I just want to peel his shirt away and rub my hands over his stomach.

"You look beautiful," he says as we stare into each other's eyes.

"Thank you." I smile, looking down at the ground, my cheeks burning as I feel Penny's eyes on me.

Chance steps forward and hands me a huge box of chocolates.

"Thank you," I say again.

"I was going to bring flowers, but well, you know." He grins, gesturing around himself at every surface covered with the flowers he's already sent.

I laugh and set the chocolates down on the side of the couch. I turn to Hayley. "You be a good girl for Penny okay?"

"I will," she says. "We're going to watch a movie and eat popcorn."

"Sounds good," I say. "Penny, call me if you need anything all right? And help yourself to anything."

"Thanks," she says. "Have fun."

I say a final goodbye and hug Hayley, then I pick my handbag up

We head out of the house.

"Hayley is a character isn't she?" Chance says as he leads me to his car.

"Oh God, what did she say?" I ask with a groan.

"She asked me if she could be the flower girl at our wedding." He grins at me.

"Oh, I'm so sorry," I say.

Chance shrugs as he opens the car door for me. "Don't be. I told her that would be just fine by me."

He closes the door leaving me momentarily speechless but insanely happy.

He walks around the car and gets in the driver's seat.

I decide to move the topic of conversation to something a little safer. "So where are we going?" I ask

"I told you. It's a surprise," he says as he pulls away.

"Bungee jumping? Skydiving? To the race track?" I tease. "I'm going to keep guessing until I get it right."

"A little tamer than that." He smiles.

"We're going to your place aren't we?" I say.

"How did you guess from that?" he asks.

"I didn't." I laugh. "I guessed from the fact we're heading in that direction."

"Clever," he says. "And yes. We are. I'm no chef, but Matt is and he's made us a lovely dinner that I just need to serve when we get there."

"Sounds good." I smile. It'll be nice to be somewhere just the two of us, so we can talk. And maybe do more than just talking.

We reach Chance's place and get out of the car.

He leads me to his front door and opens it and I step inside. "Go on through," he says, nodding at a door in front of me.

I step through the door and gasp when I come into a dining area decked out with candles on every surface. The lights aren't on in the room and the candles leave a beautiful, dim light that casts soft shadows over everything.

Chance follows me in. "You like it?"

I nod, momentarily speechless. Chance is really making an effort to do this right.

"Sit down," he says, pulling out a chair. "I'll bring dinner in."

I sit down in the seat he's pulled out and pick up the full wine glass from in front of me. I take a sip while he goes through to the kitchen. I can hear him rattling about in there and I smile to myself as I look around. Chance is definitely surprising me tonight. He's going all out, and having known him for so long, I never would have expected him to do all of this for me.

He comes back in with two plates in his hands. He puts one in front of me and sits down opposite me with the other.

I can't help but give a soft laugh when I see our dinner.

"What?" Chance grins. "Your love for fast food inspired me."

The dinner is a burger with all of the trimmings and a huge pile of fries, but it's clearly not a store bought one and when I pick it up and take a bite, juices flood my mouth. "It's delicious," I say.

"I just wish I could take the credit for that," Chance says. "But really, all I did was put them on the plates."

"Ah well, you did a good job of that." I laugh.

"That's good," he says with a smile.

We fall silent as we eat, but it's a comfortable silence and we keep looking at each other, smiling shyly, like we're just exploring the situation quietly before we have to talk about it.

"So," Chance says when we're about half way through our meal.

"So," I repeat.

"We have a lot to talk about, but first, I want to apologize again. For everything. And I want you to know your job is still there if you want it back. In my office. Not London. I can't believe I did that."

"So that's what this is about," I say. "You've realized how good of an assistant I was and you want me to come back to work for you."

"What? No. I mean yes. You're a good assistant and I would have you back tomorrow, but this is about so much more than that Sierra. Honestly, I—"

I can't hold my laugh in any longer.

Chance's face floods with relief. "You're teasing me aren't you?"

"Yup," I say, nibbling on a fry. "You didn't think I was going to make this easy did you?"

"Well no, but I kind of hoped you would." He smiles.

"Well I'll make the work part easy." I nod at him. "I don't want to come back and work for you again. It's too complicated and it would be too embarrassing coming back now."

"Ok. I get that. But if you change your mind, you only have to say the word," he says. "And Sierra, whether you choose to come back to the firm or not, nothing will change the way I feel about you." He reaches over the table and puts his hand over mine.

I look into his eyes as he talks.

"Please stay? He pleads. "Stay and give us a chance. I know the wedding was a mistake, but you weren't. I want you in my life, Sierra. Please don't leave."

"Leave? What makes you think I want to leave? After everything I said to you about not uprooting Hayley."

"You said on the phone earlier that you were planning to leave," he says.

"That's not what I meant." It suddenly all makes sense. The roses. The intimate dinner. The candles. He thought I was leaving for good and this was his way of trying to show me he didn't want me to go. My eyes fill with tears and I smile at him. "Chance I was never planning on leaving for good. Hayley's life is here. My life is here. You're here," I add the last part in a quiet voice.

Chance beams at me and squeezes my hand.

I rub my thumb over his palm. "I booked Hayley and me for a week at the beach that's all," I add. "I realized that working every hour of every day might give her a good financial start, but that's not really what she needs. What she needs is my time. To feel loved."

"So you're not leaving?" Chances asks, as though he can't quite believe what I'm telling him.

I shake my head. "No."

"Good." He smiles. "Because it's going to take me a long time to make everything up to you, but I intend to try. And I want to spend every day showing you how much you mean to me."

I smile back at him. "That sounds good. But we need to take things slowly Chance. I have Hayley to think about and I can't bring someone into her life who isn't planning on sticking around."

"I'm sticking around for as long as you'll have me, but I understand. We can take this at whatever pace you want to," Chance says.

"Well, let's start by me saying I forgive you. Let's just start over," I say.

"I'd like that." Chance beams at me.

I pick up my wine glass and drain it.

Chance gets up. He goes to the kitchen and returns with the wine bottle. He tops up my glass.

I thank him and take another drink.

He doesn't sit back down.

I look at him questioningly.

He smiles at me. "I thought maybe you might like to dance."

"Dance?" I laugh. "To what?"

He moves to the corner of the room and hits a few buttons on a sound system. "This," he says as soft jazz music fills the room. He offers me his hand.

I take it and allow him to pull me to my feet. He leads me to a sliding glass door and we step out onto a patio. He flicks a switch on as we step outside and I gasp with delight as I look around. Heaters make the patio warm enough that the chilly air doesn't bother me, but that's not what really gets my attention. Chance has strung fairy lights from the roof of the patio and it looks just like the area we danced together in at Sebastian and Kimberley's wedding.

"Do you like it?" he asks.

I nod, speechless.

"Good. Because you have no idea how hard it is to get those little lights to sit where you want them to." He laughs.

I laugh with him and he pulls me into his arms and we dance around his patio. I rest my head on his shoulder and hum along to the music, enjoying the closeness of his body against mine. I can feel my pussy getting wet and my clit throbbing as his hands move slowly up and down my back.

I pull him closer, holding him tightly against me. I don't even notice when the music ends. I just keep him held to me, swaying to the rhythm in my own head. I tilt my head back to look into his face after a few minutes.

He smiles down at me as he raises one hand and pushes a strand of hair back from my forehead. "You really are the most amazing woman I've ever met Sierra," he says quietly.

His fingers linger on my cheek, sending shivers through my body. "So kiss me then," I say, still looking into his eyes.

He lowers his head, placing his mouth to mine.

Our lips come together and my body comes to life. I don't know much, but I know I can't lose Chance again. Being with him makes me happy in a way I never thought was possible.

I move my hands slowly up and down his body as he kisses me tenderly, a kiss so full of love it almost overwhelms me. I kiss him back, sinking into him, letting him consume me. My lips are tingling, my body crying out for his touch.

I pull back from his mouth and take his hand in mine. I lead him back into the house. I pull him towards the couch and push him down. When he's sitting down, I straddle him and lean in to kiss him.

He catches me by my shoulders and stops me.

I frown down at him.

"Wait," he says.

"What is it?" I ask.

"You said you wanted to take things slowly, remember," he says.

"I did say that." I smile. "But then I felt your body against mine and I knew that wasn't something I could do." I can feel his hard cock pressing against me where I straddle him and I know I'm not the only one who wants this. Now.

"But..." he starts.

"Chance, we got married on our first date. Our second date was to your brother's wedding. I think we're past taking things slowly aren't we?" I laugh.

He laughs with me, his warm breath tickling my cheek. "I guess we are," he admits.

"You told me you're not going anywhere and I believe you. Now are you really going to try and talk me out of this after you've gone to so much effort to convince me we should give it a try?" I smile.

"Hell no." He reaches up and cups my face for a second.

I can see by the look in his eyes he meant what he said. He's not going anywhere. He's mine now and I am his. He pushes his fingers into my hair and pulls me down for a kiss

My body melts, becoming one with his.

EPILOGUE

Two Months Later

Sierra

I sit on a deck chair on the sand watching Chance and Hayley. I can't believe how much Chance has changed in these last two months. Not only has he totally relaxed around working late every night, he's even taken two months off, so we can travel. We're currently on a tiny tropical island off the coast of Mexico with our own beach house and a stretch of private beach that's just for us.

Chance is showing Hayley how to play baseball. It's definitely not something I ever would have imagined Chance doing, but he and Hayley have really taken to each other. Sometimes, I wonder if they would even notice if I wasn't here. I don't mean that in a bitter way, I think it's amazing to see the softer side of Chance, and it's so good to see Hayley having a positive male role model in her life.

"Are you ready?" Chances shouts to Hayley, getting ready to pitch the ball to her.

She holds her bat up and nods, her face set with determination.

"Okay, don't take your eyes off the ball." He takes a short run up and releases the ball gently.

Hayley hits it and whoops with joy as Chance chases after it. Hayley begins to run to first base.

Chance throws himself at the ball, landing stretched out on the sand. He gets up and runs towards Hayley, but she's already safely at second base.

She puts her tongue out at him and he laughs.

I study Chance for a moment, taking in his shorts, his tanned legs. He wears a casual t-shirt and a baseball cap. I still can't believe how much he's mellowed out. When he suggested this trip, I half imagined him sitting on a beach in his full suit, his laptop on his knee as he frantically typed emails. I'm still half waiting for Sandy to pop up and him to start giving her instructions.

"Okay. Ready for another pitch?" Chance asks Hayley, pulling my attention back to their game.

Hayley nods eagerly and goes back to their batting spot. Chance runs up and Hayley hits the ball again, harder this time. She starts running immediately, but instead of chasing the ball, Chance chases her. She hears him coming and squeals and runs faster, but he catches her easily. He scoops her up, throws her into the air and catches her.

"Chance no, you can't do that. It's cheating!" Hayley is saying, but she can hardly speak for laughing.

"Are you sure? Because I think it's in the rules you can do this." Chance grins as he throws her into the air again.

I can't help but smile as I watch the two of them.

"It's not," Hayley insists.

"Ah, okay then, you better get running," Chance says, releasing her.

She takes off and makes her first home run. She whoops and jumps into the air.

Chance goes wild, clapping and cheering and she runs back to him for a fist bump.

My phone buzzes on the little table beside me, making me jump.

It's a text from Sebastian. *The baby is here. Can you Facetime us or are you too busy having fun?*

I laugh to myself and shake my head. As if we wouldn't be able to fit in a phone call to check in. I'm so happy for Sebastian and Kimberley.

Watching Chance and Hayley still laughing and messing around makes me feel so happy. "Chance," I shout, putting my hand up to shield my eyes from the sun.

He doesn't even look in my direction. He and Hayley are too engrossed in their game to hear me.

I get up and head towards them.

Chance turns as I approach them, but before I can speak, he runs towards me and picks me up with one arm. He throws me over his shoulder and runs around the bases, tickling my ribs as I go.

I scream and laugh.

Hayley joins in, laughing and pointing at us.

"Hayley, help me!" I pant out between laughs.

She runs to my aid and Chance scoops her up in his other arm, throwing her over his other shoulder.

She squeals and giggles. Her little fists pound on his back as she laughingly demands we be released.

After a few minutes, Chance puts us down.

I look over at Hayley and grin. "Now," I say.

We run towards Chance and knock him off his feet, the three of us landing giggling in the sand. I sit across Chance's hips and Hayley kneels behind his head, holding his wrists down.

"Okay, okay, I give in. You girls win!" Chance laughs.

Hayley holds her hand up and I high five her, then I remember why I came down here in the first place. "Come on," I say, getting up and helping Chance to his feet. "We need to pop into the house and Facetime Sebastian. Kimberley had her baby."

CHANCE

We head up to the beach house, a tight little unit of three. I have always been worried about the idea of having children, not sure I would know what to do with them, but spending time with Hayley has shown me that actually, I have nothing to worry about on that score. We have a lot of fun together and she's a great kid that's showing me how much better life can be when you just let your hair down and enjoy the moment.

This vacation is exactly what we all needed. It's brought us together as a family, because even though it's only been two months since Sierra and I had our first official date, it feels like longer. It feels like we're permanent and that we always have been.

"Chance," Sierra says, looking at me with a frown.

I realize she's holding the phone out to me and I take it. "Sorry, I was just thinking about something."

"What?" she asks.

"I'll tell you after the call," I say.

She gives me a look that says she won't forget to ask me about it.

I hope she doesn't, because I really don't know if I'll dare tell her what I was thinking without prompting. I hit call and the three of us sit huddled around the phone.

Sebastian takes the call and appears on the screen. "Hey guys, how's the vacation going?"

"Perfect," Sierra and I say together.

"It's awesome, but Chance cheats at baseball," Hayley says.

"I don't doubt it." Sebastian laughs. "But I bet you still win right?"

Hayley nods and gives him a big cheesy grin.

"How's Kimberley and the baby?" Sierra asks.

"They're both doing well," Sebastian replies as he moves his phone and Kimberley appears in the shot.

She looks tired, but flushed and well. She gives us a little wave.

Sebastian moves the camera again and a tiny baby in a bassinet fills the screen.

Sierra and Hayley both make aww noises.

I smile. "She's beautiful bro. What are you calling her?" I say.

Sebastian and Kimberley appear back on the screen.

"Aria," Kimberley says. "It's the name we picked for Carl, but of course he turned out to be a boy."

"Where is he?" I ask.

"With your parents. They're on their way," Kimberley replies.

"So how was it?" Sierra asks. "The labor I mean."

"Not too bad. Easier than the last one. Sebastian cried more than I did this time." Kimberley laughs.

"That's so not true," Sebastian says, nudging Kimberley. "And Chance if you say anything about that, I'm ending this call."

"If I get you wound up today, Sierra will kill me," I say. "But you know it'll come."

"Ah, I don't even care." Sebastian laughs. "When you have your own kids, you'll understand."

"Yeah and you'll finally understand what the word *tired* actually means," Kimberley puts in.

"Oh God, of course, sorry Kimberley. We should go," Sierra says.

"Oh no, that's not what I meant," Kimberley insists.

"I know, but you'll have visitors soon and I'm sure you'd appreciate a bit of rest before everyone appears," Sierra says.

Kimberley smiles gratefully and we say our goodbyes.

I end the call.

"Can we go in the pool for a bit?" Hayley asks.

"Sure honey, go grab your swimsuit from your room," Sierra says.

Hayley runs away cheering.

Sierra turns to me. "So what were you thinking about earlier? You said you would tell me after the call," she says.

I nod my head, suddenly nervous. I can feel my palms sweating and my mouth is suddenly dry. "I-I wondered how you would feel about you and Hayley moving in with me when we get home," I say. "I know it's quick, but I love you and I want to spend every moment with you."

Sierra doesn't respond.

I hurry on, "I understand if it's too quick. Just say the word and I'll back off."

"It's not that," Sierra says. "I'd love nothing more than us all living together. But I don't know how Hayley would feel about it. I know she loves you, but I'm not sure how she would feel about leaving our home. I'll talk to her though and see how she feels about it."

"See how I feel about what?" Hayley asks, coming up behind us.

Sierra looks at me and I nod at her. She crouches down beside Hayley. "How would you feel about me and you going to live with Chance when we get home from our vacation?" she says.

Hayley goes quiet and looks from Sierra to me and back again. "Do I get my own room?" she asks.

Sierra looks at me and smiles.

"Oh yes," I say. "And we'll decorate it any way you want."

"Then yes." She nods.

She gets up and runs to the door like this isn't a big deal. "Come on," she calls. "Last one to the pool is a loser." She darts away.

Sierra starts to follow her.

I grab her wrist and spin her to face me. "Is that a yes, then?" I ask.

"You heard the boss. It's a yes." She smiles.

I lean in to kiss her and everything feels right with the world.

Sierra pulls away from me with a grin and darts off. "Looks like you're the loser," she taunts me as she reaches the door.

I run after her, not making any real effort to catch up.

She jumps into the pool with Hayley.

I watch them splashing each other and laughing, I know one thing for sure. I'm not the loser here. I am most definitely the winner.

CALLIE

I can feel my happiness bubbling up inside of me as I step away from the crowd of students. College has been a long, hard road, but I've finally graduated and I'm clutching my diploma as proof of that.

I begin to make my way through the people gathered in the large hall, our friends and family who have come out to support us today and celebrate with us. I scan the crowd looking for Matt. Finally, I spot him and run towards him.

He spots me coming towards him and his face breaks into a wide beam as he rushes forward to meet me.

We come together. He picks me up and spins me around. I clasp my hands behind his neck and even when he puts me back down I don't let go of him. Instead, I stretch my face up to his and kiss him. His lips have the effect on me that they always do. They make my insides tingle, making me forget everyone around us and sneak off alone together.

Matt pulls back slightly and smiles at me. "I'm so proud of you," he says quietly.

I raise up on my tiptoes and kiss him again. A long, passionate kiss that makes my pussy clench. Matt is so getting it tonight. I pull away from the kiss, suddenly remembering where we are, and that my grandparents were behind me when I spotted Matt. Being around him, even after three years together always has this effect on me. I guess that's true love. It doesn't fade away over time; it only gets stronger.

"There's someone I want you to meet," I whisper to him.

I already know my grandparents are going to love Matt almost as much as I do. How could they not when he makes me so happy?

MATT

I am so proud of Callie on her graduation day. I know how hard she has worked to graduate with honors and she's worked full time all the way through college too. No amount of me telling her I would pay her tuition fees broke through her determination to do this alone. And now all of her hard work has paid off.

I hold her in my arms a moment longer after she tells me there's someone she wants me to meet, just looking into her eyes that shine with excitement as she looks back at me. She's so beautiful when she smiles.

"Come on," she says, gently disentangling herself from my arms.

She turns around and an older couple stand off to one side looking at us. Callie leads me over to them. "Matt, this is Dorothy and Samuel, my grandparents. Grandma, Grandpa, this is Matt."

I shake hands with Samuel and hug Dorothy.

"It's nice to finally meet you Matt. We've heard a lot about you," Samuel says.

"All good I hope," I say.

Dorothy smiles and nods. "Oh, definitely. You make Callie very happy, I know that much."

"Not half as happy as she makes me," I smile.

This gets a look of approval from both Dorothy and Samuel.

"Because of how happy she is, we've even decided to turn a blind eye to the fact you're both living in sin," Dorothy says.

I feel my cheeks heat up.

Callie shrieks from beside me. "Grandma! You can't say that... we're doing no such thing!"

Dorothy laughs. "Sure you are. You think your grandpa and I don't know you're living with Matt? We're giving you our blessing Callie, for goodness sake just accept it. We know things are different now to how they were when we were courting."

"That word *courting* being one of them," Callie laughs. "Seriously though, thank you. It means a lot that you're giving us your approval." She hugs each of her grandparents in turn.

They hug her back fiercely. It's clear they dote on her.

"Why don't you join us tonight for dinner son?" Samuel asks me. "We're taking Callie out to celebrate her graduation and we'd love to have you along,"

"Oh no, I couldn't impose like that. But thank you for the offer though," I say.

"Nonsense," Samuel replies. "You're family now and I won't take no for an answer."

"Then I guess I'd better say yes then." I grin. "Thank you."

A friend of Callie's comes over and congratulates her. She introduces her friend to her grandparents.

While they're talking, Callie nudges me. "They really like you." She smiles widely.

"Good," I say, leaning down and kissing her again. "Because I'm happier with you than I've ever been in my life and I'm not planning on that changing."

"It won't," Callie whispers. "I've never been happier either and I couldn't have done all of this without you."

I kiss her again and then her friend says her goodbyes and the four of us walk towards the exit ready to go for a family dinner.

KIMBERLEY

I'm so tired I could easily fall asleep anywhere right now, but I want to stay awake. I want to be with Sebastian and Aria. I want to be awake when Carl gets here. Sebastian is watching me and I am suddenly conscious of the absolute state I must look. I can feel my hair sticking to my head with sweat from the labor. I give Sebastian a self-conscious smile. "What?" I ask.

"I was just thinking how good you look." He smiles.

"You need to go to the eye doctor," I joke.

"No, I don't," he says. "Kimberley you have given me the best gift anyone could have ever given me. A family. And you have never looked more amazing than you do right now."

I can see him getting teary eyed again and I force myself into a sitting position. I lean forward and pull him into my arms.

He holds me tightly for a moment and then he releases me with a shaky laugh. "God, I'm getting so soft," he says. "I just have to think about the kids and I'm a marshmallow."

"Me too," I agree, feeling the tears in my own eyes.

"I don't think it was necessary for you to tell Chance and Sierra that I was crying while you were in labor though." He grins.

"Oh, it *so* was." I laugh.

He leans forward and brushes his lips over mine. "You're lucky I love you enough to not want to get you back."

I pull him closer and kiss him again, a full kiss that makes my heart beat faster as I feel the warmth of love filling me up. "I'm so happy right now."

"Me too," he agrees.

"Let's try Matt again," I say. "And I promise I won't tell him you're a big softie."

He nods and hands me his phone.

I find Matt's name and press call. I hang up when the call goes through to his voicemail. "He's not picking up," I say.

"Oh of course he isn't," Sebastian says. "It's Callie's graduation ceremony today isn't it? I forgot all about it."

"Of course, I forgot too. Well, he'll call us back eventually."

Sebastian takes the phone from me and sends Matt a text.

I am glad for this moment as it's just the three of us. I turn my head to look at my perfect little daughter.

The peace doesn't last long though. The door opens and within seconds, the room is full of people and I find myself swamped with kisses and hugs.

SEBASTIAN

The door to the room opens and a crowd pours in. My parents, Kimberley's parents, Bernie and her boyfriend and finally, Carl.

I bend down and pick Carl up. "Hey buddy, are you all right?" I ask.

He nods uncertainty. This must all be a little overwhelming for him.

I move to Kimberley's side and Carl reaches his arms down to her. She takes him and gives him a hug and he settles down beside her.

I go to the bassinet and pick Aria up. I move to the side of the bed and sit down. "Carl? This is your sister, Aria. Are you going to be a good big brother?"

Carl nods, looking at the little bundle wrapped in white.

I pull the blanket down slightly and hold Aria out to Carl. "Are you going to give her a kiss?"

Carl leans forward and plants a rather sloppy kiss on Aria's head. This gets an aww from the full room and Carl beams proudly.

"You're going to be an amazing brother, Carl," my dad says, stepping closer to Carl and rubbing his head.

My mom steps closer to me. "May I?" she asks, nodding at baby Aria.

I nod my head and she takes her.

My dad takes Carl and Bernie's boyfriend joins their little group. Bernie and Kimberley's parents are crowding around my mom, fussing over the baby.

I smile at Kimberley and she smiles back at me.

Her eyes are almost closed, but she looks content, happy.

She's not the only one. Never in my wildest dreams did I imagine a time when I would be this happy, when I would have a family to call my own with the only woman I have ever loved. I shuffle closer to Kimberley and squeeze her hand.

She squeezes back and her eyes close. They fly open again when the door opens.

Matt and Callie burst in and she is still in her graduation robe.

"What are you two doing here? You're supposed to be at your graduation ceremony," I say.

"Like we'd miss this," Callie says. She steps around me and hugs Kimberley.

"The ceremony is over," Matt adds. "We're just on our way to have a celebratory dinner with Callie's grandparents," Matt says.

"You'll have to pretend like you two don't live together." I laugh.

"They know and they've given us their blessing," Matt replies.

I laugh and clap him on the shoulder. "That's great, bro."

Callie has hold of Aria now.

"It won't be long until she starts getting moody you know." I laugh.

"She's not the only one," Matt says. "Now if you'll excuse us, we really do have to get going. Callie wanted to pop in and see the baby, but we've left her grandparents downstairs, and they might stop approving of me if we leave them down there all day."

"Of course, go." I nod. "Thanks for stopping by."

Matt and Callie's departure seems to remind everyone that Kimberley is exhausted and we could really use some alone time. So, one by one, they all file out with hugs, kisses and promises to visit tomorrow.

I turn to Kimberley when everyone else has left. "It's funny how it's all turned out isn't it? There's me and you, childhood sweethearts who no one ever really believed would go the distance with two children. Chance who has been married to the job since he was old enough to leave school, actually taking time off to spend with his girl. And Matt, the sensible one who everyone thought would be the first to get married, still happily living in sin with his girl."

"That's what keeps life interesting. People surprising you," Kimberley says sleepily.

"Yeah, I guess you're right." I stand up and kiss her forehead. "I'm going to go for a walk down to the cafeteria and get some coffee, so you can get some sleep okay? I'll be back soon."

Kimberley doesn't argue. She's already asleep by the time I finish talking.

I brush her hair back from her face and take one last look at Aria who is also asleep, her eyelashes laid over her little white cheeks. I'm so tempted to pick her up and hold her, but I hear Kimberley in my head, telling me if I wake her up, she'll kill me. So, I slip out of the room.

I don't go to the cafeteria though. I don't want to be that far away from them. Instead, I sit down in a chair in the corridor to wait for Kimberley to wake. I still can't believe this is real, that after all of those years of telling myself I didn't love Kimberley, that I finally let myself just admit that I love her more than anything else in the world and have the life with her I've always wanted.

The End

Want to read Chance's brothers' stories too?

Read Matt's here:
Reckless Entanglement

And Sebastian here:
Untangle My Heart

COMING NEXT... SAMPLE CHAPTERS

TEMPTED BY THE CEO

PROLOGUE

Opal

When I see the time, I stand up quickly from my desk. Mr. Connell, CEO of Asima Assets Management, and my direct boss, has a meeting in half an hour that's been flagged as important. I have been told to remind him half an hour before the meeting is due to begin. I don't want to be even a minute late, because Mr. Connell is the kind of man who notices little things like that.

I walk briskly from my desk to Mr. Connell's office although there isn't much space to cover for me to get there. As Mr. Connell's personal secretary, I am the last line of defense between him and all of the people who want to take up his time. Most people understand that a polite no means just that. But at only five foot three, I'm not exactly intimidating. Yet, I am charged with keeping the people he doesn't want to deal with in the moment away from him.

Working directly for Mr. Connell for two years now, I still find myself nervous every time I have to go into his office. My palms start sweating and I can feel my heart speeding up a little, but over the years, I've learned to hide my nerves well, so no one would ever know I was anything but calm and confident.

I take a half second to study the door while I take a deep breath. The door is a simple light oak bearing the company logo - a circle of red encasing the blue lettering of the company name, the capital letters in a matching red – and a nameplate that reads *Robert Connell, CEO.*

Wiping my palms down my navy blue pencil skirt, I tap on the door. Mr. Connell calls for me to enter. I step inside, a bright smile plastered across my face.

"What is it, Opal?" Mr. Connell asks, looking up from his computer and smiling at me. Mr. Connell is in his early fifties. His black hair is just starting to turn grey around his temples but his grey colored eyes are as sharp as ever. He wears his age well like a good bottle of wine, and he has no shortage of admirers, both in and out of the office.

"You have a meeting in half an hour with Brian Meyers," I say. "You asked for a reminder half an hour before he is due to arrive."

"Thank you." Mr. Connell smiles. "Please call his secretary and confirm."

With a nod, I step back out of his office, pulling his door closed behind me. I mentally add the phone call to my daily to do list and hurry back to my desk. I'd like to call it my office, but truth be told, it's more of a cubby hole. My desk is tucked back into a slight recess a couple of yards down from Mr. Connell's office. It's private enough and the corridor is usually quiet enough for me to work uninterrupted, but I would love an office so I could kick the door shut and keep the world out. It would kind of defeat the purpose of my job though, as a big part of my job is greeting Mr. Connell's associates and potential new clients.

Sitting down at my desk, I turn to my computer. I look up the number for Brian Meyers' secretary, noting that her name is Suzy and I dial her number.

The call is answered on the first ring, "Suzy Hayes, secretary to Mr. Meyers," she says.

Efficient. I like that. "Hi Suzy. This is Opal Collins. I am calling to confirm the eleven o'clock meeting between Mr. Meyers and Mr. Connell of Asima Assets Management."

"Mr. Meyers is currently on his way to the meeting," Suzy assures me.

Thanking her, I end the call. I look at my list of tasks for the day and I know instantly, I'll be working late tonight again. There's no way I can get through all of this before five. I see that tomorrow's schedule is just as busy, so I can't put off any of my tasks. I sigh and pick up the phone to make the first of many calls I have to make.

I have just ended a call when the light on my phone flashes to tell me Mr. Connell is calling me. "Hello," I say, picking up the phone.

"Opal, have you confirmed the meeting like I asked you to?" he says.

"Yes, Mr. Connell," I reply. "I didn't want to disturb you, but the meeting is still going ahead as planned. I would have only felt the need to disturb you if the answer had been a no." Oh God, have I fucked up? Has he been expecting me to let him know either way?

"That's fine. I just wanted to check you'd called already. Mr. Meyers is an extremely difficult man to pin down and to be honest, I was half expecting him to cancel this appointment."

I instantly feel better. I haven't made a mistake. Whew.

Mr. Connell goes on, not waiting for an answer, "Please hold all of my calls until after my meeting. See Mr. Meyers in when he arrives and then make sure I am not disturbed under any circumstances for the duration of the meeting," he says.

"Yes, Mr. Connell." I resist the urge to tell him I would never allow him to be disturbed during a meeting. I don't really know a lot about Mr. Meyers or his company or why he's having a meeting with Mr. Connell. But it must be important if Mr. Connell feels the need to point out something so obvious to me. I have to admit I'm curious about the whole thing. As Mr. Connell's personal secretary, I usually get to know what his meetings are about, but this one is like some top secret mission where I haven't been told anything really, except Mr. Meyers' name and his company name.

I shake my head slightly. I don't have time to be distracted by trying to work out exactly what's going on here. It's none of my business and if at some point down the line, I do need to know about it, then I know I will be told.

Tending to another two calls, I fend off three calls for Mr. Connell, taking down the details and promising to pass them on once Mr. Connell is out of his meeting. While typing up some letters, I hear footsteps coming along the corridor. I look up from my typing to see a man I don't recognize, making his way along the corridor towards me.

A little on the short side, he looks to be about the same age as Mr. Connell, although the years haven't been quite as kind to him. He has a little bit of a paunch and his hairline is receding. He's wearing a very expensive looking suit.

I wonder briefly if it's to compensate for his hairline. I tell myself to stop being a bitch as I stand up and extend my hand. "Mr. Meyers, I presume?" I smile.

He shakes my outstretched hand. He has a firm grip, but his palm is slightly sweaty. His sweaty palm makes him seem nervous, as does the slight twitch in his right eye. He smiles at me as he nods his head curtly, but the smile doesn't reach his eyes.

"I'm Opal Collins," I greet him. "Mr. Connell's secretary. If you'd like to follow me please." I step around in front of Mr. Meyers and lead him towards Mr. Connell's office. My own palms remain dry, my confidence buoyed by the nerves of Mr. Meyers.

Knocking on Mr. Connell's office door, I push it open when he shouts for me to come in. I stand back and gesture for Mr. Meyers to enter. "Your eleven o'clock Mr. Connell," I smile. "Would you like any refreshments brought in?"

"No thank you," Mr. Connell replies, answering for both men as he stands up to shake Mr. Meyers' hand. "That will be all, Opal."

With a nod, I step out of the office and gently close the door. I'm tempted to remain in place and see if I can work out who the mysterious Mr. Meyers is and why he clearly doesn't want to be here, but I decide against it. It would be the height of unprofessional and I would be fired instantly if caught.

I return to my desk and try to forget about my curiosity. It doesn't take long for me to lose myself in finishing typing up the letters.

When I hear footsteps approaching, I steel myself for an argument when I tell whoever it is that Mr. Connell is unavailable but I relax when I see it's just Jessie, one of the other secretaries.

She's practically skipping along the corridor, her auburn curls bouncing on her shoulders as she approaches. She's grinning, a wide grin that makes her eyes sparkle.

I know that look. It's the look that says she has something particularly juicy to share with me. I feel a mild streak of annoyance run through me at the interruption for something that clearly isn't going to be about the business, but I decide to hear Jessie out.

Reaching my desk, she plonks herself down in the chair opposite mine. She's so excitable she reminds me of a puppy. All she needs to do is start panting. "Guess what," she says, her eyes shining with excitement. She can't keep still on the chair, her whole body shifting constantly. She reaches up with one hand and twirls a curl around her finger.

"What?" I ask, smiling despite my earlier annoyance as I feel myself getting pulled into her excitement.

"You have to guess," she insists.

I roll my eyes. "You got a promotion?"

She shakes her head.

"You were right about Martha from accounts sleeping with the mailman?"

"Yes, I was right about that, but that's not it," Jessie gushes.

"God Jess, I don't know. Have you won the lottery or something?"

Jessie laughs, a musical sound that is infectious.

Now, I feel the last bit of annoyance leave me, even though part of me wants to shake her to get her to cut to the chase.

"Honestly Opal, you are so bad at this game," she says shaking her head.

Even my lack of game playing skills don't keep her down for long though and she grins again as she finally reveals her news, "Word is that the ever elusive Brett Connell, Mr. Connell's son, has just pulled into the parking garage."

"Rightttt," I say, drawing the word out into a question. How the hell would I have guessed that? And why is Jessie so excited about it? I mean I know Brett is rather elusive to say the least, but still. After two years of working directly for Mr. Connell, I have never met nor spoken to his son. But then is that so weird? Brett's a grown man. He probably has his own life that doesn't involve coming to see his father at work.

I've heard plenty of rumors about Brett. Everything from him being the black sheep of the family who did time in juvie as a teenager to him being a recluse who refuses to leave his home. The truth is probably neither of those things. Obviously, the latter isn't true, or he wouldn't be here now. And if the former was true, Jessie would already have spilled all of the details of it to me.

None of this really helps to explain why Jessie is so excited about this though. Or why she thinks I will care about the

news. "Seriously Opal, try to at least pretend to be excited."
She laughs.

"Ok," I say. "I'm excited. There... I pretended. Now why is
this something you're so excited about?"

"Now, I am offended." Jessie tries to give me a pout, but is
unable to stop herself from smiling. "I'm just shocked you
even have to ask. But then in your defense, you haven't seen
Brett before, have you?"

I shake my head.

Jessie fans herself with her hand, as she gets up from the chair
and starts to walk away. She turns back to grin at me. "I'm
going to go and pretend I need to take the elevator somewhere, so I can be there when he gets out. Once you see him,
you'll understand my excitement. Brace yourself Opal. You
are about to see the most beautiful man who ever existed."

Laughing softly and shaking my head, I can't help but wonder
what this guy is going to look like to have her that excited
about his arrival. I mean is he made of gold or something?

I guess I'm about to find out. Jessie has only been gone from
my desk for a couple of minutes when I hear the ping of the
elevator arriving and I know it'll be mere seconds before the
door opens. It doesn't necessarily mean it's this Brett guy, but
a couple of seconds later, I hear Jessie laughing in a flirty way.
I smile to myself as I picture her tossing her hair back and
laughing hysterically at something that is, at best, mildly
amusing probably.

Pretending to be fixated on my computer screen, although I
have completely lost track of the figures, I wait just a few
seconds. I then realize I'll have to start over again. *Great.*

Thanks for that Jessie. I can't put all of the blame on Jessie though. I should have had more sense than to let myself get pulled into the conversation, but Jessie is a good friend and I have to admit I enjoy her cheerful personality. It keeps office life interesting.

I glance up without moving my head when I hear quick, quiet footsteps approaching. I don't see much. I don't let my eyes linger in case he catches me looking at him. All I see is a flash of a grey suit and that the man is tall. I mean everyone is tall compared to me, but he must be well over six feet tall. He has a definite presence, a confidence that I can almost feel as he moves towards me, and despite myself, my breath catches a little in my throat.

Keeping my eyes glued on my screen again, until Brett is almost at my desk, I know it would be rude not to acknowledge him at this point. His cologne fills my nostrils, a woodsy, spicy scent that should be overpowering but somehow isn't. As I turn my eyes up to look at him, I try to forget Jessie's words and her excitement.

I smile up at him, flashing him my polished, customer service smile. It freezes on my face when I finally allow myself to look at Brett properly. Jessie wasn't exaggerating about Brett's looks. In fact, calling him the most beautiful man I would ever see actually feels like she's sold him short a little bit.

The man is that fucking hot.

He looks like he's around thirty five, certainly no older than that. With thick dark hair in a trendy style that manages to look tousled and casual like he hasn't made any effort with it at all, and yet perfectly styled and in place at the same time. Staring at his full, thick hair, I imagine myself pushing my fingers into it as his lips move to meet mine. It would be silky soft, the kind of hair you want to touch constantly and can never get enough of.

I force myself to look away from his hair, feeling my cheeks turning pink as I shake off the image of my hands in his hair, his lips on mine. It turns out that looking away from his hair is a mistake. It had been distracting, but it has nothing compared to his eyes. They're the color of caramel, a warm greenish brown that makes me melt inside. His eyes are so mesmerising that I can't look away from them, and the longer I look at them, the more detail I see. The green is flecked with tiny specks of lighter brown, a color that is almost gold the flecks catch the light and sparkle as though they really are tiny pieces of gold leaf floating there in his eyes.

The gold flecks make me think of my earlier thought when I wondered if the man was made of gold or something. It turns out I wasn't wrong, except that next to him, gold would look like cheap copper. Something to be tossed aside in favor of the much better thing beside it.

Brett clears his throat.

Now, I feel the slight flush on my face when I realize just how long I've been staring at him. Wow, Jessie was so right about him. I should have been more prepared, so I could play it cool.

Instead, I stare at Brett and I realize with horror that I'm still staring at him. Even as my mind screams at me to look away from him, I just can't quite bring myself to do it. And to make matters worse, my mouth is still frozen in my fake, customer service smile. My cheeks are actually starting to ache from the smile. I must look like I have a damned coat hanger wedged in my mouth.

Could this get any worse? I mean I guess I could have set him on fire or something, but on a normal scale of things, where arson isn't a player, then no, it really couldn't be going much worse at all.

I finally manage to force my eyes away from him. Well, not away from him exactly, but I manage to stop staring into his eyes like some extra from a bad soap opera, and at least move my gaze down to this mouth. It's no safer really, all I can think of when I look at his lips is how they will taste sweet. Now, I don't think I'll ever be able to speak again.

Brett smiles at me and there's nothing fake about his smile. It makes his eyes light up and it takes everything I have not to stare into them again. His teeth are straight and white, like something from a toothpaste commercial and I can't help but wonder absently if he's ever done any modelling.

"Hi. I'm Brett Connell," he says as he holds his hand out to me.

Suddenly, I realize with horror that he wants to shake my hand. But my palm is disgustingly sweaty by now and I can't exactly wipe it down on my skirt without him noticing. I shyly extend my hand and he envelopes it in his large, dry hand. I wait for him to pull away in disgust, but to his credit, he shakes my hand like it's normal to touch a stranger's sopping wet palm and his expression doesn't change. He must know the effect he has on women. There's no way he can look like this and not know about it. He probably had been expecting my palm to be wet. I don't know if this makes it better or worse, but I don't waste any energy worrying about it.

As my hand is enveloped in his, I feel a bolt of lightning burst through my body, lighting me up from the inside out. It's as though his touch wakes something up inside of me. The lightning bolt spreads through my body, heading straight for my clit which tingles and makes me press my thighs together.

Brett releases my hand.

I hear myself make a quiet *ahh* sound. I hope he hasn't heard it. If he has, he doesn't comment on it, but he's not going to is he? He probably thinks I'm his father's charity project, like he's doing some sort of outreach where he employs mental cases or something. I mean I am sweaty, mesmerized by him, and still completely mute. What else is he supposed to think? Even if he knows he has an effect on women, he can't think this is normal.

"I'm here to see Robert Connell," Brett adds.

I find it odd that he refers to his father so formally and somehow, that breaks the spell and I find my voice again. "Mr. Connell is in a very important meeting right now." My voice comes out low and breathy. It's not like my normal voice, but I kind of like it. It's kind of sexy and at least it's not shaky or weird. "He doesn't want to be disturbed, but you're more than welcome to wait. I can show you to an empty office if you would like?"

Brett frowns ever so slightly and shakes his head.

During our whole exchange, his eyes have been on me, on my face, on my chest. I should be either offended or flattered, I can't decide which, but instead, I'm mortified. Of course, he's watching me. He's probably waiting for the crazy girl to jump up and try and kiss him or something and he wants to be prepared so he can duck away in time to avoid me.

"No thank you," Brett says.

I don't know whether I'm relieved he's going to leave, so I can stop embarrassing myself, or whether I'm gutted he's going to leave because I'll most likely, never get another chance to see him again.

"I'll see him now," he adds. He half turns and starts towards his father's office door.

I jump to my feet. "You can't go in there!"

Brett glances back over his shoulder and gives me a lopsided smile. "Is that so?" he grins.

His grin makes my pussy clench and my heart race. I nod, momentarily mute again. "Yes... I," I start, but I'm too late.

Brett's hand is already on the door handle of Mr. Connell's office and before I can utter another word, he pushes the door open and goes inside.

Oh God, I am in so much trouble here.

Stepping back behind my desk, I sit down heavily. I have barely sat down when Brian Meyers storms out of the office. I open my mouth to say something to try and make this better, but he doesn't even glance in my direction as he marches past me. I can see his face is full of thunder and I don't know what to do to fix it. There's really no fixing this.

I might as well just start packing my things because I can't see Mr. Connell accepting the fact that I let someone disturb him and pissed off Mr. Meyers like that. I put my face in my hands for a moment, resting my elbows on my desk. I swallow hard, trying to work out what I'm going to say to Mr. Connell when he demands an explanation for this. I can hardly say I was so distracted by Brett's looks that I was too late to stop him when I realized his intentions.

Goddammit. I've screwed up so big here and for what? A smile from a handsome stranger. Was it worth it?

The worst part is that a big part of me thinks it was.

Pre-order the book here:
Tempted By The CEO

ABOUT THE AUTHOR

Thank you so much for reading!
If you have enjoyed the book and would like to leave a
precious review for me, please kindly do so here:

Tangled With The CEO

Please click on the link below to receive info about my latest
releases and giveaways.
NEVER MISS A THING

Or
come and say hello here:

ALSO BY IONA ROSE

Nanny Wanted

CEO's Secret Baby

New Boss, Old Enemy

Craving The CEO

Forbidden Touch

Crushing On My Doctor

Reckless Entanglement

Untangle My Heart

Made in the USA
Middletown, DE
11 September 2021